Malignant Memory

Malignant Memory
© 2017 by Barbara Paterson
eBook ISBN: 978-0-9953327-1-3
Paperback ISBN: 978-0-9953327-0-6

No portion of this book may be duplicated or used in any form, by any electronic or mechanical means (including photocopying, recording, or information storage and retrieval), for any profit-driven enterprise, without prior permission in writing from the publisher. Brief excerpts may be shared subject to inclusion of this copyright notice:
© 2017 by Barbara Paterson. All rights reserved.
Additional copies of this book may be ordered by visiting the PPG Online Bookstore at:

PolishedPublishingGroup

shop.polishedpublishinggroup.com
Due to the dynamic nature of the Internet, any website addresses mentioned within this book might have been changed or discontinued since its publication.

Printed in Canada

ACKNOWLEDGEMENTS

I have been blessed with many people who have loved and supported me throughout the writing of this book, too many to mention. I am especially grateful for the wisdom and care offered by my husband, George, and my sisters Laura and Brenda. A special thank you to my First Nations friends who experienced the impact of residential schools in a deeply personal way. In their generous and courageous sharing of their stories with me, they provided insights that were critical to this book. Lastly, I am profoundly grateful for the influence of my grandmother, Loretta Paterson. It is her story that provides the loose fabric of the book.

MALIGNANT MEMORY

Barbara L. Paterson

PROLOGUE

Once I knew a man called Close. I knew him as Close for almost three decades before I discovered that it was not his real name. He had been christened Charles but no one called him anything but Close.

It was Close, himself, who told me the story of his name; it had been given to him at conception. Close's father was frantically penetrating his wife in spirited coitus when his penis fell from its destination. He gave one last desperate thrust into his wife's vagina, spilling Close's beginnings as he did so. He cried out, "Close call" as he ejaculated.

I know nothing about the circumstances of my own conception. My parents were tight-lipped about such things. I am confident, however, that my beginnings involved a secret, a secret of such enormity that it forever shaped who I was to become.

I am a guardian of others' secrets.

I am the person that others tell their secrets to; I am the confessor.

The secrets revealed to me are not admissions of joy or happiness. They are not whispered declarations of a wanted pregnancy, a wedding, a trip, or an impending award. They are confessions of deception, revenge, betrayal, wrongdoing, and deceit. I am an ongoing witness to the torture of remorse, guilt, self-reproach, shame, and humiliation that are the legacy of such secrets.

Strangers, acquaintances, friends, and kin, all ages, both male and female, have confided in me since I was a child. The tellers divulge their secrets to me as if they were placing their confidences in a vault for safe-keeping. They make their deposit in me, knowing that I will not repeat what I have been told.

Malignant Memory

Secret tellers approach me wherever I go. They walk across rooms just to speak to me. They divulge their stories as they sit beside me on planes, trains and buses, in waiting rooms, and cafeterias. They whisper their revelations at parties, concerts, church services, and other public gatherings. A few have followed me to breathe their confession through the bathroom door as I evacuate.

Both strangers and those known to me have approached me to guard their secrets. Strangers choose me as the guardian of their secrets because they know it is unlikely that we will meet again. When on a rare occasion I encounter them once more, they are embarrassed to see me—as if I had betrayed an unspoken pact by not remaining estranged.

Secret tellers who are my friends, family, or neighbours generally avoid me for a time after they have revealed their secret. I suspect they fear I will see only their confession when I meet them again. They remain cautious and guarded once a renewed relationship is forced by events. They watch me closely for signs of a change in the way we relate to one another. Our relationship resumes once enough time has passed and they detect no difference in the way I interact with them.

Sometimes, the relationship with familiar secret tellers never recovers its original bonds. I am an unwanted reminder of what they prefer to remain hidden. Some secret tellers look upon me forever more with animosity because the reminder is so painful. I have lost important relationships in my life because of this.

The responses to telling their secrets are as individual as the secret tellers themselves. Some respond with visible relief, as if the secret has been a cancer, eating away their soul. Banking their confession with me is surgical treatment. They have dethroned the tyrant that ruled their lives. They grin and giggle to themselves at their emancipation.

Others have nurtured the secret, enjoyed the pleasure of something that is theirs alone—known only to them. They zealously guard their secret until something happens that convinces them that the secret threatens their freedom, their livelihood, or their most precious relationships.

They tend to divulge their confession in pieces, as if telling the entire story at once will be too much of a loss. These secret tellers grieve for the loss of their secret after they have confided the entirety of their story.

Prologue

Some secret tellers appear shocked by their words, as if the secret had been so well-hidden that even they were not fully aware of its existence. These secret tellers are masterful deniers. They lock the secret in the recesses of their consciousness until they no longer recall its existence. They open their eyes wide and their pupils dilate as they acknowledge the validity of the secret, perhaps for the first time. Their defences disintegrate. They are confused, dazed, as they make their exit from me. Sometimes they say, "Well, now I guess I have some decisions to make," or "It's out there. I guess that makes it real."

Occasionally, the impact of disclosing a secret is so dire that secret tellers retreat into depression or other mental illness. Some leave the people they know and recreate their identity elsewhere. Others find alternative means of exodus.

I have retreated to my bed after some particularly enigmatic and troubling secrets. I remain under the shelter of the covers for many days, refusing food, lost in the subconscious world of shadow pictures behind my eyelids. I remain in that state until the secret is firmly deposited into my unconsciousness, and I am recovered sufficiently to begin again. My loved ones observe the pain and fatigue I experience. They try to protect me. They intervene, telling someone who is making their way to me in a crowd, "She needs to be alone right now."

I confess that I too have at times tried to escape secret tellers. I have feigned sleep to discourage conversation. I have pretended I was needed elsewhere, but the secret tellers always find a way to make a deposit into the vault that is me.

To be eyewitness to the angst and fallibility of human kind is a cruel destiny. I feel the secret tellers' anguish as acutely as if their stories are my own. I have been brought to my knees by the power of the emotions I experience as secrets are divulged. I am regularly overcome by my own impotence to bring healing to those who suffer because of their secrets. The confessions I hear have caused me to question my own existence, my faith in others, my values.

My journey in becoming a guardian of secrets has been a convoluted one. I have learned lessons about guarding secrets along the way, only to have to re-learn them later on with another secret, another secret teller. I have made many mistakes. I have judged. I have betrayed confidences. I have thought I needed to give advice.

Malignant Memory

It is one secret in particular that haunts my days and nights. It has grown in magnitude as the years have passed. I can no longer push it away from my consciousness. Like a lumbering, ungainly giant, it tramples my dreams and disturbs my waking moments. I recreate the secret—and the events that explain it—over and over again in my mind. I see his tortured face, her eyes filled with pain. I think of little else.

The people involved in the secret are dead, gone from this world for over half a century. They no longer hold me to the promise of secrecy. I offer you this story to unburden my soul of this wretched, malignant tale. I must liberate myself before the secret destroys the little peace that is left to me.

I have embraced this secret, nurtured it, and contained it for most of my life. I am asking you to help me relieve the anguish of the secret by guarding it for me, helping me to release it by sharing it with you.

Are you willing to guard the secret, to protect it for me?

All right.

I will tell you.

You need to know that the secret I am about to divulge will not make much sense to you if I relate it as decontextualized from the larger story that birthed it, that caused it to have the impact it did in my life. The telling of the story will take some time for it has many twists and turns, ebbs and flows. Please be patient with me as I tell it.

I will start, then, at the beginning.

CHAPTER ONE

BEGINNINGS

The first secret given to me to guard was told to me by my father, George Anderson. I was eight years old. My mother told me to fetch him from the barn for supper. I wandered into the barn. Father was sitting on a hay bale, his head cradled in his hands. He turned to face me when I called to him.

Father had just had his 38th birthday. He was thin, almost emaciated, but his forearms and leg muscles were strong and sinewy. His hair had turned grey almost a decade before; much of it was missing from the top of his head. His grey-blue eyes were moist with tears. He leaned slightly toward me, studying me closely. It was clear he was going to talk to me, to share a confidence.

Father was a man of few words. He grunted his responses to most questions. He rarely initiated conversation. His limited discourse centred on the farm, mainly the ills of the livestock and the failure of the crops. I could not recall us having a conversation about anything of depth before this time.

I was suddenly overcome with foreboding. I was both fascinated and petrified about what was to come next.

I sat beside him on the bale and waited. He gulped once, then again. He cleared his throat. Then he began.

Father said, "I have been a coward. Everything I have done since I became an adult was to escape something. I did what I did because I couldn't face my guilt. Or my sadness. So I escaped. And every escape has resulted in a catastrophe."

I did not understand. I wanted more explanation. Father did not continue. I stayed silent, letting the secret find its hiding place in me.

Malignant Memory

Father arose abruptly. We went into the house for supper. We never spoke again about what he had revealed.

People in his hometown of Kingsford had referred to my father before World War II as a man destined for greatness. He was a stellar student, a superb athlete, a devoted son to his widowed mother, and hugely popular. People would often hold up Father as the exemplar of what a good man should be. He was loved and affirmed by everyone he knew. Such adoration bred in him a confidence rarely seen in one so young. It also made him ill-equipped for what he would experience later in life.

In 1940, Father enlisted in the army to go to war. He was 18. He was to take a train to Montreal to await his orders for overseas. He later wrote his mother that others on the train were solemn and quiet. He had whistled and sung to himself, grinning widely. He caught a glimpse of himself in the train window. He winked mischievously at his reflection. He was filled with excitement about the possibilities that lay before him. Why, he could become a war hero decorated for extreme courage in the face of mortal danger! He could become a legend in his time! He could be promoted to General! Anything was possible!

Five years later, Father returned to Kingsford, disenchanted with the world he once knew. He was outraged about the promises that had been made to him before the war by his priests, his teachers, and the government. He had seen firsthand the devastation that men can create. He was wracked with guilt because of the wickedness in which he had participated. He could scarcely believe he was capable of the horrific crimes he had committed against other humans. He had seen things that would haunt his dreams for all the years to come. He was filled with angry despair that the people of Kingsford seemed eager to forget the atrocities he had witnessed.

After the war, Father was a changed man. He was eerily quiet, only speaking when others asked direct questions and then he answered in as few words as possible. He rarely smiled. He lost interest in fun of any kind. The townspeople whispered, "Whatever happened to George in the war? He's not the same George."

Soon after his return to Kingsford, Father was joined by his new bride my mother Emily and my oldest brother, an infant at the time. Father and Mother had not seen each other since their wedding

Beginnings

in England eleven months before. Father had never met his tiny son.
Mother had met my father at a dance hall, when Father was stationed in England. I see photographs of her from this time; she is beautiful, svelte, laughing. I see no resemblance to the dowdy, grim, stocky woman I knew as my mother.

Mother often told me, "George danced divinely, just like in the movies, when we met. I fell in love instantly." I was incredulous whenever she repeated this story. It was difficult to believe that the dour, wordless man I knew as my father was a romantic figure. I never saw him dance.

Father made only one comment about his marriage. It was when I was ten. He said, "I didn't love your mother then, and I don't love her now. I married her because I wanted to escape thinking about the war. I realized almost right away that I would never love her. By then she was pregnant with your brother." I was not shocked by these words, even at my young age. I had never witnessed my parents being demonstrative with one another. They rarely spoke to each other, but neither did they quarrel. They lived a life of desolate truce, married only for the practicalities it offered them.

There were three boys born in the first three years of their marriage: my oldest brother and twin boys. The financial strain of a growing family meant that Father could no longer offer money to support his mother as he had done throughout the war years. My grandmother Henrietta Anderson, or Andy as the townspeople of Kingsford called her, subsisted on a meagre World War I widow's pension. She barely had enough money to manage without Father's support. Father observed his mother becoming thinner and thinner, as she saved money by not eating. He felt guilty. He dealt with his guilt by seeing Andy only rarely—and then only when she precipitated a visit.

Mother was miserable. She was ill-equipped for the cold Canadian winters, the drudgery of housework and childcare, or the scathing resentment of a mother-in-law who could no longer rely on the fixed devotion and support of her only son. Mother blamed the proximity to Andy as the reason why she was depressed. To substantiate her claim, she provided my father with a daily, detailed listing of the incidents that confirmed that my grandmother hated her.

Father craved a new possibility for his existence, an escape from the tedious and conflict-filled life he experienced post-war in Kingsford. It was at this time that he came across the novel Tarry Flynn. He fell in love with the poetic image of farming that the book offered. Even now, I wonder whether our futures might have been shaped in different ways if he had read a book that more accurately and less romantically portrayed the toil and uncertainty of farming.

Over the next year, Father cultivated a vision of himself as a farmer. The dream flourished until he was certain that farming was the only true pathway for his life. He overlooked the fact that he had never visited a farm. He did not consult those who knew farming. He turned a deaf ear to the cries of his wife who protested that both of them had been city folk all their lives; they knew nothing about farming.

Father convinced himself that farming far away from the city and people he had known all his life was the only chance he had to regain his assurance and vivacity. This uninformed and unresearched dream prompted him to purchase a pitiful parcel of land in Northern Manitoba. The farm had been for sale for several years before Father bought it. Three generations of farmers had been unable to secure a livelihood on that land. The land could not support crops or livestock. The soil designated for crops and gardens was mostly clay. The century-old wooden house on the farm teetered dangerously to one side. Water damage was evident in every room. An ominous crack, the size of a man's fist, ran from the cellar to the roof. The barns were equally dilapidated. They were ramshackle and full of vermin.

In preparation for what he was certain would be a charmed future, Father spent several weeks discerning a name for the farm. "It has to be the right one," he proclaimed. "A name is an omen of what the farm will be." He painted a sign that would be hung at the entrance to announce the farm's new moniker, "Paradise Regained."

I was born shortly after my parents moved to the farm. Father invited the neighbours to a victory celebration of food and drink. "Elizabeth's birth is a sign," he declared. "It speaks to the good fortune and good life we will have on this farm." The neighbours sipped their cider and looked at one another in sombre, knowing ways.

Mother produced a new infant almost every year. When I recall my childhood, I see her as perpetually exhausted, incessantly disappointed in life, wearing torn coveralls that barely concealed her current or recent pregnancy. By the time I was 14 years old, I had nine

Beginnings

brothers whose ages ranged from three months to 18 years old. Mother hemorrhaged, nearly died, after her last pregnancy. My youngest brother was her last child.

Gender roles were clearly prescribed on the farm. The boys' job was to do farm chores once they were no longer toddlers. My job as the only girl was to care for the younger boys, do the laundry, clean the house, darn holes in socks and coveralls, and cook the meals.

I grew to love cooking, but it was difficult to feel motivated by other household chores. I had little interest in them. To wash floors and dishes only to have to rewash them shortly afterwards seemed a fruitless and thankless task. To numb the monotony, I read books while I cleaned. I became adept at washing the floor with one hand and a book perched in the other.

The role I found most taxing was caring for my brothers. My brothers were a tsunami of testosterone. They were noisy, unruly, and unmanageable. Their pranks were endless. They burned rubber boots in the furnace just to see if rubber would burn. The house filled with putrid, black smoke that did not clear for weeks. They made two-year-old Peter swallow a bottle of my mother's perfume. The perfume was one of Mother's few prized possessions. She had brought it with her from England. It was mostly alcohol. Peter became horribly sick. He swayed on the chair, too drunk to hold a sitting position. Father had to take him to the hospital three hours away to have his stomach pumped.

I was held directly responsible whenever my brothers' pranks had an outcome deserving of attention. My parents would deliver long tirades to persuade me of my guilt and lack of responsibility.

"Why didn't you watch them more closely? Were you reading your books again? You always have your head in books. All we ask is that you help us by looking after them and keeping them out of trouble. We work so hard trying to keep a roof over your heads and food in your mouths. Is it too much to ask that you help us by watching your brothers?"

Money was a constant concern on the farm. My father was easy prey for salesmen who assured him that the latest shiny tractor, fertilizer, weed killer, or combine would guarantee the farm's success. Initially, banks were eager to loan him the money for such purchases.

Malignant Memory

Later, they would be even more enthusiastic about demanding their money be returned to them with interest.

The clay soil proved to be the breaking point. Tilling the heavy earth was arduous. It took until late June for the soil to warm up from the winter. By that time, all our neighbours had planted their crops and were watching new green shoots sprout. After a rain, the land on our farm would drain slowly. Plants often rotted in the puddles that remained. No matter how much my father mixed the land with sand, added chemicals to it, or poured manure into it, it remained inhospitable to living things. Even weeds could not prosper on that land.

Our neighbour, Fred, said often, "It's the strangest thing. All around is rich, fertile land known for growing everything, but this one patch of land, your farm, is clay, pure clay. You can't do nothin' to fix that much clay. It's hopeless."

Someone painted over the sign at the farm's entrance. The anonymous culprit renamed the farm "Paradise Lost." It was then that Father declared himself finished with his dream. With unrelenting crop failures, livestock dying, and crippling debt, he finally acknowledged that the farm was destined to be a failure. He spent hours sitting on the front steps, staring into space as my brothers worked tirelessly to save the remaining crops and animals.

One spring, my oldest brother, Jonathan, found a dead calf in the barn. The calf had mysteriously strangled herself with the rope used to tie her to a stall. "She committed suicide," he told me sardonically. "Even the animals will do anything to get out of here."

Father wrote his mother, Andy, faithfully every week. He omitted any details of our lives that would reveal that his dream had failed. His letters told of prosperity on the farm. He exaggerated the extent of his meagre bounty. One hundred bushels of wheat became 10,000. He hinted at outrageous wealth, not extreme poverty. He told outright lies about the fine clothes Mother and the children wore and the many parties we hosted for the neighbours. His letters were masterpieces in deceit, so craftily penned that even Father found himself believing what he had written.

I do not know how Father justified in his letters that he never sent his mother money. I am unclear why my grandmother did not question his providence when no money came her way. I suspected that Andy had

Beginnings

such a long history of believing everything her adored son said, that she did not question it.

It was one afternoon in April, shortly after my 14th birthday, that Father came into the house bearing a letter. The letter was from Andy. We were sitting at the kitchen table, ready to begin lunch.

Father read the letter aloud.

"Dear Son, I have come into a considerable fortune. My dear sister, Helen, has left me some money in her will. It is a great deal more than I ever expected. It means that for the first time in a terribly long time, I won't be strapped for money.

I would like to do two things with this unexpected blessing. One is to send you some money. A money order is enclosed. Please do whatever you like with this.

The other is to have Elizabeth come to live with me until she finishes high school. I have become concerned that your village does not have the resources such a clever child needs. She could attend Saint Theresa High just as you did. Elizabeth will receive an excellent foundation for university there. If Elizabeth could come to me in June, we would have a few months to get to know one another. She could make friends before she starts school.

I promise to take good care of Elizabeth when she is with me. I have enclosed a separate money order for Elizabeth's train ticket. Please write and let me know when I can expect her to arrive. I am sending you, Emily, and the children all my love. Mother."

There were a few minutes of stunned silence after Father read the letter aloud. He caressed the money orders with one hand. He stared at me, as if to judge my reaction.

It was then that he stopped to read aloud the amount typed on the money order addressed to him. My parents wept without constraint. The money would not pay off all their debts, but it would assuage the creditors for several months.

"Can you believe it?" Mother asked incredulously. "We are going to be all right. It's a miracle." Father laughed. We children stared at him. We had not heard him laugh for a very long time. Father began to fantasize aloud about selling the farm and pursuing his latest escape plan, opening a restaurant in Quebec City.

I paid no attention to the money mentioned in the letter, only to the part about my going to Kingsford for three years. I could hardly

Malignant Memory

imagine my good luck. One of the twins, my brother, Tom, jeered at me. "How come you get to leave and not one of the boys?" I merely shrugged. I thought it was a dream come true. I was going to escape. No more housework. No more evil children. No more feeling guilty when I stole time to read. It was going to be heaven.

I felt a kinship with my grandmother that I couldn't explain. We children had never met her. She had planned to visit many times, but my father would dissuade her with some fib: The younger boys have scarlet fever, they are still contagious. It's one of our busiest seasons, we would have no time to visit.

We had received many kind gifts from Andy over the years. Every birthday, she would send us a little money to buy what we wanted as well as a card with a note just for us. She called me Sweet Pea in her letters. Once she wrote, "Sweet Pea, you are so special to me. You are my hope, my joy, and my blessing."

I had always been curious about my grandmother, asking my father many questions about her. "How did she meet Grandfather?" "What games did she play with you when you were young?" "What does she like to do?" I learned soon enough that my father would pretend he had not heard me. He would deign to answer only if I asked him factual questions that required one-word answers.

"How old is she?"
"Fifty-six."
"Did she have any children other than you?"
"No."
"How many brothers and sisters does she have?"
"Four."
"Did you meet them?"
"Some. Go make bread. That's enough questions."

I learned about Andy mainly from my mother. She referred to Andy as "The Beast." Her stories about her mother-in-law emphasized Andy's worst attributes.

There was the matter of my birthday. I was born at 11:50 PM on April 2nd. Andy's birthday is April 3rd. My mother claimed that The Beast wrote her, "You couldn't keep your legs together for 10 more minutes so Elizabeth and I could share the same birthday?"

Mother told me that when he was a teenager, Father joined the

Beginnings

youth group in the local Protestant church. His father was a patient in the TB sanatorium. Father and Andy had little money. There was rarely much food in the house.

Father hadn't joined the Protestant youth group because of any theological leanings. He became a member simply because he was hungry. The Protestant youth group provided free lunches and hot chocolate every Saturday.

Father did not tell Andy that he had joined the youth group, but she found out. A neighbour blabbed that she had seen Father at the group. My mother claimed that the night Andy discovered Father's deception, she beat him until he could barely stand. Mother said, "She was not upset that he was with the Protestants, even though she is a staunch Catholic. It was because every kid who went to the youth group was poor. Everyone in Kingsford knew that. Andy was furious that people in town might realize that they were poor."

It was clear that Andy was not a one-dimensional woman. She could be terrifying but at the same time, kind and affectionate. I was so eager to escape my plight on the farm that I forced myself to be confident that her loving side would govern her behaviour toward me.

My parents spent much of the evening discussing Andy's dictate to send me to live with her. They were caught in the web of deceit that Father had so carefully woven in his letters. How could they say they could not afford for me to leave because they would have to hire a housekeeper? He had written about their excellent nanny and cook. And yet how could they let me go when there would be no one to cook the meals or look after the housecleaning and laundry?

My parents told me at breakfast the next morning that I could go to Kingsford if that is what I wanted. "We could tell Andy that you didn't want to go," Mother said hopefully. I shook my head. I could hardly wait to leave.

I bid good-bye to my mother and brothers in the last week of June. They were crying. The younger boys clung to me, begging me not to go. I was surprised at the tug I felt in my heart as I hugged each one.

Father brought me to the train station. He shook my hand as if we were passing strangers.

Malignant Memory

"Study hard," he said.

I was about to climb the stairs to sit on the train, when he reached out suddenly to grab my wrist.

"I am letting you go because I have no choice." He wiped his eyes with his coat sleeve and then turned abruptly to walk away from me.

I waved frantically to my father as the train started its journey. He did not turn around. I watched him from my seat at the window until I could no longer see him. The train huffed and chugged toward Kingsford: toward a new, more carefree life.

CHAPTER TWO

CONTRADICTIONS

It took over four hours to arrive at Kingsford. I could barely sit still during the train ride. My skin felt as if a billion ants were crawling on its surface. My breath was quick and hard. My heart pounded. I looked out the window, forcing myself to concentrate on the landscape unfolding as we passed by. The train seemed to crawl at a snail's pace.

Wooooooo, woo, woo, woooo! The train horn shrilled as we approached the Kingsford station. The brakes screeched to a halt, metal grinding on metal. Andy was waiting for me on the platform.

I recognized her immediately from a photograph we had of her on our mantel back home. She was like my father in stature, tall and gaunt. Her features were sharp, her nose prominent and beak-like. She was not unattractive, merely severe.

Andy's dated attire was that of a prim, middle-aged maiden without prospects for love. She wore a white starched blouse, navy skirt, matching wrist-length navy gloves, and a white pillbox hat with navy netting that veiled its brim. Her greying brown hair had been meticulously curled with bobby pins. Small, equally spaced, snail-like curls framed her face. She was unusually pale. Two circles of rouge were painted on her cheeks, accentuating her pasty complexion.

Andy bellowed out to me from the opposite end of the platform, her hand forming a cup around her lips. I could not make out what she was saying because there was too much noise from the commotion of passengers, greeting those who had come to welcome them. The clamour reminded me of the daily symphony provided by chickadees, swallows, and blue jays on the farm. Suddenly I became acutely aware

Malignant Memory

of how far away I was from my family, and how little I knew of Andy. I felt tears sting my eyes. I was filled with longing for my family and dread of what was to come.

Andy waved in my direction with such ferocity I thought she might become airborne at any moment. To a casual onlooker, she appeared joyously unrestrained and boisterous. One who studied her more thoughtfully would have concluded that such exuberance was calculated and contrived. Her eyes were dark. Her forehead was crinkled in aversion. The muscles in her cheeks danced spasmodically as she attempted to control her tension.

Andy greeted me with a hug. She angled her body to form an A-line so that we touched only at the shoulders.

"I am glad you're here." She said this as if it were a question. We walked, suitcases in hand, for several blocks from the train station to Andy's home. She chatted incessantly, moving seamlessly from one thought to another.

"This is a railroad town you know. Although the railroad isn't here anymore. I think it closed in 1943. Or was it '45? No matter. It was several years ago. People in Kingsford are fiercely loyal to the railroad, even though it's gone. They even hold an annual Railway Days parade every summer. Townspeople dress up as railway figures and make parade floats in the shape of railway cars. Now, the main industry in the town is the pulp mill. The sulfur smell from the mill is disgusting, but you'll soon get used to it. I won't have you complaining about the smell. After all, the pulp mill provides an income for people in this town. They would be dead poor without that mill. I live in a railroad worker's house. It's little and brick, built around the 1850s. There is a cemetery at the end of the street where I live; that's where your grandfather was buried. He had tuberculosis, TB, you know. Stayed in the sanatorium for five years. Big Gulp is buried there too. We called him that because he used to make a gulping sound as a kid whenever he was scared. People in Kingsford love to give nicknames. I think it's their way of telling people they are one of them. You'll have one soon enough, a nickname. Me, I'm 'Andy'. It's short for Anderson. Sometimes, I can't recall what people's real names are anymore; we have always used the nickname. Like Big Gulp. Even on the tombstone, he is Big Gulp. I'll be darned if I can remember his real name. I love the baby graves in the

Contradictions

cemetery. They look so sweet—little stone angels weeping over them as they lie there. It would have killed me to lose a baby. Did you know your father was a blue baby? He was so small when he was born; he was blue in colour. We kept him in a dresser drawer with a hot water bottle for weeks."

I wondered to myself if Andy had ever heard of periods; there were no breaks in her monologue. Neither was there space for me to ask questions or to make comments. She asked nothing about me or my family.

I was used to silence in my life on the farm. My brothers were often outside when I worked in the house. My parents were not conversationalists. I found Andy's relentless talking exhausting. It was a relief when we encountered one of her neighbours; only then did she stop talking at me.

Kingsford had a population of over 30,000, but it seemed as though Andy knew everyone we saw. They were excited to see her. They were anxious to tell her their news. "Andy!" they exclaimed, "It's so good to see you."

Andy stopped to admire their gardens. She commented brightly about the warm weather. She made affirming comments about the neighbours' attire or haircuts. She inquired about their health, their children, their work, and their pets. She deflected their queries about herself with such dexterity that the inquirers did not seem to notice that their questions remained unanswered.

"So, Andy, how have you been feeling? Did you get the flu that's been going around?"

"Did you know Min broke her hip?"

"Is that right? I hadn't heard. Poor Min."

In every interaction, Andy proudly introduced me as her granddaughter.

"This is Elizabeth, my granddaughter. She's going to stay in Kingsford until university."

Many of Andy's neighbours stopped to hug her. I noticed that she tolerated their touch but did not reciprocate, her arms held tightly against her ribs until the embrace was over. Her mouth twisted slightly at the corners as if she found their touch repugnant.

Just as she had described, the railroad worker's house where

Andy lived was old, little, and brick. The unassuming house was entirely without decoration or embellishment. It was square-shaped with a flat, tin roof. There were only two windows, one at each side of the front door, each configured oddly in a different size and shape. Some of the mortar between the bricks was cracked, receded and falling out of the joints. Many of the bricks were crumbling. A tiny garden of sparsely planted daisies to the right of the front door bloomed hopefully.

Andy opened the front door to the small rectangular living room. The room was dark and stuffy. It smelled of wintergreen. The furniture was crowded and mismatched. There was an ornate green couch with wooden griffin heads at each end. Two stiff-backed chairs, one orange and one red, crowded the couch. A small, dark wood table was placed at one end of the room. A blue and white oval rug made from rags lay in the middle of the room. Over 50 photographs, mainly of my father, adorned the walls in a display of jumbled memories.

Andy pointed to a small room immediately adjacent to the living room.

"That one is yours. Mine is right across the hall from yours," she said. "You go unpack. I'll make dinner."

My bedroom was small, the size of a large closet. The bed was an army cot that Andy had salvaged from a veteran, a friend of hers. A knitted blue blanket covered the cot. The linen case on the sole pillow had been hand-embroidered with tiny rosebuds. It read, "Elizabeth." Andy smiled when she saw me looking at the bed. "I knitted the blanket and made the pillow just for you. So you'd feel at home." I was touched by her thoughtfulness.

A photograph of my father as an infant adorned the wall behind the cot. I was fascinated by the abundance of blonde curls on his head in the photo. I wondered when his hair had decided to elude him. Had it decided that it had made such a splendid display in his early years that there was no more need of it later on? Or had the torment of war devastated his follicles, causing his hair to abandon him forever?

The bedroom was gloomy, painted a dull, dark green. Only a filigreed pink lamp on a small table provided a hint of light in the room. One-third of the room was taken up by a massive oak roll-top desk. The desk was almost as tall as me. "It was your grandfather's," Andy told me when she saw me fingering the grooves of one of the hand-carved drawer handles. "Watch you don't scratch it."

Contradictions

There was a china doll sitting on the bed. She had a slightly open Cupid's bow mouth, thick painted eyelashes over her bright blue eyes, and dark cascading curls. She was dressed in a pink and white dress with white pantaloons. Both feet were covered by tiny white leather shoes. I thought she was the most beautiful doll I had ever seen.

I looked questioningly at Andy. "That's my doll, Betsy," Andy said. "Your grandfather gave her to me before we were married. I thought you might like her company."

I came into the kitchen after unpacking my belongings. Andy invited me to have a seat at the small white table while she cooked supper. I watched in horror as she washed two pork chops under the tap. She slopped oil into the frying pan while she talked cheerily and without pause about her plans for our first week together. She placed the chops in the pan and turned the heat of the element to high. Smoke choked us in seconds.

I was hungry, but I had to force myself to eat the unpalatable food. Not only was the food tasteless and overcooked, but the house reeked of foul-smelling smoke from the pulp mill. I remembered Andy's caution on our walk to her house and was silent about the odour.

In the following weeks, I was to learn little about Andy from Andy. She made it obvious that she did not like to be asked about her life, often refusing to answer my questions. I contented myself with learning about my grandmother from my observations and the comments of others.

Andy did not resemble any grandmother I had heard or read about. She was not demonstrative. She touched me only in cursory ways, to straighten my hair as she passed by me in the narrow hallway or to call my attention from a book I was reading. Andy had referred to me in endearing terms in her letters to the farm. She only called me Elizabeth in person. She never complimented me directly, preferring instead to inflate my attributes when speaking to others about me. "She is the cleverest one in the family." "She is so good and kind, almost a saint." I did not recognize myself in her descriptions of me to others.

Andy's mannerisms were both peculiar and perplexing. She insisted that the lights remain on in every room of the house at all times, even in the daylight. She kept the bathroom door slightly ajar when she was on the toilet or washing at the sink. She became visibly agitated

Malignant Memory

when I attempted to close the door. "Leave it alone. I like it open." She never bathed in the tub, preferring to sponge herself standing at the sink.

Andy checked the closets every night before she went to bed. She would open the closet door gingerly, as if she expected to be devoured by a nameless monster who resided there. She would peer cautiously into the opened closet for several minutes, poking at the contents with a broom handle before forcefully closing the door with a loud bang. She would repeat the ritual several times over before she moved onto the next closet.

Andy rarely slept. She retired to her bedroom after midnight each evening. I could hear her moving about in her bedroom, muttering to herself, throughout the night hours. She was up and dressed before 5:00 each morning.

Andy went to Mass every day, no matter what was happening or how she was feeling. Mass at St. Francis Church was held at 6:30 on weekday mornings and at 7:00, 9:00, and 11:00 AM on Sundays and Holy Days. She attended every Mass offered. When I asked her why she attended Mass so often, she merely shrugged.

Andy detested cooking. She polluted what she cooked with her hatred for the art. She cooked everything, from eggs to roast beef, in a cast iron skillet with oodles of oil on the highest heat. She never used the oven. "Too much trouble to clean," she declared. She never consulted a recipe. She did not use spices, but was liberal with salt. She refused to cook all vegetables with the exception of canned peas and creamed corn. When I offered to do the cooking, she barked, "It's my job. I'll do it."

At night, I dreamed of meals prepared by myself in the farm kitchen, of pies and cakes, of fresh milk, vegetables and fruit picked that morning from neighbouring gardens, and of meat that had been butchered by my father. I lost weight steadily. At the end of my first month in Kingsford, my clothes hung on me.

Andy was absurdly frugal, reusing her teabags at least six times to save money. Yet she could be inordinately generous at times. She gave me a weekly allowance. It was the first time I had money of my own. Once she overheard a girl in the neighbourhood make disparaging remarks about my clothes. I wore mostly coveralls, passed down from my older brothers. The girl sneered, "You look like you are back at the farm. Girls in the city wear dresses, not coveralls. Don't you have any

Contradictions

dresses?" Andy's wardrobe had remained the same for forty years. She often commented that it was a waste of money to keep buying new clothes, but she bought material to sew dresses for me.

Andy was an impatient and tortured sewer. She kicked her peddle sewing machine whenever she was frustrated with her efforts. Whenever she made a mistake, she yelled out, "Darn machine. It never works properly when you need it to." She pieced strips of material to hide where she had cut the fabric by mistake. She created darts where they were not intended to be, in order to deal with fitting issues. She secured hems with tape and staples. Despite their imperfections, the dresses were an improvement on coveralls. I was pleased by her gift.

The neighbours told me how lucky I was to have Andy as a grandmother. They said that she was the kindest person ever, that she was a wonderful neighbour. Some told me that she was the most interesting person they knew.

"I love her. She's so interesting to talk to."

"I always feel lucky to have spent time with Andy. She's lovely."

I watched Andy with her neighbours. I saw that she focussed on them, rather than herself. She offered little information about her health, her plans, or her concerns, but she spent hours prying such information from them. She acknowledged the neighbours' answers to her questions with nods or murmurs until they stopped talking. Sometimes she said, "Interesting" or "Oh my." She never followed up their responses with a question. She simply changed topics. I learned a valuable lesson in observing Andy's interactions with the neighbours: if you want to be considered a great communicator, listen more than you talk.

Andy had a different communication style with me. She did not ask me questions about my day, or about what I liked or thought. She just talked and talked and talked at me. If I interrupted her deluge, she would stare at me for a few seconds as if I had suddenly materialized from outer space and then continue talking.

Andy was often out of the house when I was home from school, leaving me alone for long periods of time. She apologized that she was away so often. She explained that she was busy caring for others. She implied that without her intervention, the world would collapse.

Malignant Memory

Andy's acts of caring for her neighbours were endless. She mailed cards every week to extend wishes of sympathy, recovery, or congratulations. She cleaned houses and weeded gardens for those who could not. She paid extended visits to those she deemed as lonely. She delivered groceries for those who were infirm. She shared baked goods from the bakery with those who were grieving or desolate. She knit and crocheted baby clothes for the new babies in the neighbourhood. She coordinated fundraiser teas and bake sales to provide proceeds to neighbours who were destitute. She led a daily prayer group to pray for the souls of neighbours, government leaders, the priests, the Pope, and heathens.

Andy pointed to a portrait of Jesus that hung in the living room as justification for her busyness. "He insists that we care for others." It was difficult to believe that the pale, tortured-looking, effeminate man in the picture was capable of issuing any command worthy of submission. He looked more like a hairdresser frustrated with a client's attempt to cut her own hair than someone who could enforce benevolence.

Andy did not appear to derive any joy from doing what she described as "her Christian duty." She executed tasks of caring with calculated, frenetic precision, as a series of mandatory acts that she abhorred. She often complained loudly about the "demands of others" for her time and attention. She would return from her neighbours' homes with stories of how inept, ignorant, or inconsiderate they were.

"That stupid Mrs. Clarkson. She told me that she knew her son was going to heaven because he had a smile on his face when she saw him lying in the coffin. She didn't even know that the undertaker would have arranged his face that way. And besides, there's no way that man is going to heaven. He was evil."

"You wouldn't have believed how dirty their house was. They used the closet floor for their cat to poop on, and they hung their clothes in that closet. I scrubbed the closet last month with everything I had in me. It was clean when I left. They promised me that the cat wouldn't use it as a litter box anymore. Then today I return and find that darn cat using the closet as a bathroom again!"

We rarely had visitors at Andy's house. Some neighbours would drop by with a mission to borrow sugar or to tell Andy news, but Andy never invited people to a meal or for a visit. The telephone rang only rarely.

Contradictions

When someone telephoned, Andy kept the conversation short. She pretended to be in a hurry to go elsewhere.

Every night after supper, Andy and I walked around the town for an hour or more. Kingsford was a pretty town, a cared-for town. The locals tended their lawns and gardens faithfully. Their houses were brightly painted and pristine. Flowers of all kinds bloomed mightily on the boulevards during the summer months.

On our evening walks, Andy would often point to the small wooden and brick houses lining the streets and say, "Never forget. Behind each of those doors people are living a life that cannot be seen from the outside. Don't think you know people just because you talk to them. Most people have secrets that they keep locked away from others." She did not offer to tell me about her own secrets.

My favourite times with Andy were when she told stories about people in her past. She was a colourful and entertaining storyteller. None of her stories featured herself.

Almost every day, Andy would take me to the cemetery at the end of the block. We began our visits with my grandfather's grave. Grandfather had died before the war. What I knew about him prior to coming to Kingsford was almost nothing. Father rarely spoke of him. I knew that Grandfather was an appliance salesman in a local store. I knew that he had died of tuberculosis. I knew that he had never made much money. Everything else about him was a mystery.

Andy would reveal new facets of my grandfather each time we stood at his grave.

"His feet were unbelievably smelly. Really, it would make you gag. He couldn't smell them. His nose had been injured in the war, the First World War, so he didn't have any idea that the smell was as bad as it was. But he knew it bothered me. He tried all sorts of powders and creams. Nothing worked. He even saw a doctor about it. Once, as a joke, he wrapped his feet in flowers, trilliums, before he came to bed. He said, 'Now I will smell better.' I laughed and laughed. He didn't know that trilliums smell bad too. They are a beautiful flower, but they stink."

"He had pet rabbits. Angora rabbits. I can't remember when he didn't have them. He was fascinated by them—by everything about them. He visited them in their cage every morning, noon, and night. He taught them tricks. Like how to use their paw to signal when they wanted out of the cage. He was so tender toward them. He would stroke them for hours. Once I caught your grandfather singing to a rabbit who was lying in his arms like a baby. He loved those rabbits. And they seemed to love him right back."

Gradually over time, my grandfather assumed a real persona in my imagination.

At each visit to the cemetery, we walked around, stopping to stare at the tombstones of people Andy had known. She told me stories about the people buried there. She was particularly fond of tales that revealed the pathos and paradoxes of life.

"That's Emily's grave. Her husband, Lionel, was so mean to her. Emily was only seventeen when she married Lionel. He was forty years old. And she was in love with someone else. John Scully was his name. That's his grave over there." Andy pointed to a tall granite stone to our left.

"Emily and John were so much in love. Everyone who saw them together knew it. But John's sister had consumption, tuberculosis. In those days, they used to think that once someone got TB, everyone in the person's family would get it and die. Her father said no to her marrying John. He was not going to risk his daughter catching TB. Emily married Lionel within a year. I suspect she thought her life was over when she couldn't be with John. She didn't care that Lionel was horrid. She died of TB two years later. Imagine that! Her father thought he was protecting her from getting TB, and she got it anyway."

"That grave to your right, it belongs to my friend Elsie Morrow. Her baby girl was buried beside her. Elsie was forty-six when she had her baby. They thought she would never have children. It was a great sadness in her life that she was barren. I always told her that miracles happen, that she shouldn't give up hope. She knit so many outfits for the baby when she was expecting. I used to tease her that the baby would need to change outfits every hour just to wear them all. The baby was the sweetest little thing. They named the baby after me, Henrietta—a horrible name for a baby if you ask me, but it was their decision. We called her little Hen. Little Hen had blonde curls. She smiled all the time. Elsie and her husband Jake adored her. But little Hen died at six months of age. She got a disease. I think it was meningitis, I'm not sure, now. Elsie was devastated. She kept asking me, over and over, 'Why would God do that to me? I had accepted

Contradictions

my fate as a childless woman. Why would he give me little Hen and then take her away? And make me watch while she died in pain and suffering?' I had no answers for her."

I loved Andy's stories. I grew accustomed to her strange ways. I enjoyed my time alone to read when Andy was ministering to others. But I missed my brothers' antics and the peaceful seclusion of our farm. I wrote letters home every week. My parents rarely wrote back. Their few short letters focussed mainly on the weather and the state of the crops. Occasionally, I received a drawing or a few words from one of my brothers; these just made me feel more alone.

Over time, I accepted my new life with Andy with all of its contradictions. I wrote in my journal:

"I can't figure Andy out. She doesn't want to talk about her life and who she is. She has strange habits that I don't understand. Why does she have to leave the bathroom door open all the time? And I swear she doesn't sleep. Ever!

I thought Andy would be one of these lovely grandmothers you read about—the ones who love you no matter what and bake you cookies just to see you smile. But Andy's not like that.

Andy may not be a soft and cuddly grandmother, but sometimes she is very kind. I like the stories she tells me.

I am going to focus on when she's kind. I am going to appreciate her stories. I will try to ignore her strangeness and her bad cooking. I am going to be grateful, not resentful. I won't expect her to be something she's not. I will just love her."

It seemed so simple when I wrote these words. Little did I know then that loving Andy would prove to be a daunting assignment.

CHAPTER THREE

AN EDUCATION

I began attending St. Theresa Catholic High School for Girls in September. I stood on the sidewalk in front of the massive brick building for several minutes on my first day, afraid to enter. I was intimidated by the size of the school. It seemed enormous in comparison with the one-room school I had left.

I walked slowly up the school stairs. A larger-than-life sized all-white statue of Jesus Christ stood at the entrance with his arms outstretched. He seemed to be welcoming me, to say it was going to be fine; I'd be all right. I looked closely at the face. He looked sad, as if he alone was privy to the grief I would experience there. I hesitated. Then I forced myself to open the door and begin my life at St. Theresa's.

The school was old. It had been built in the early 1900s. It was not a particularly remarkable building. It resembled most institutional buildings of its time, brick on the outside with wooden floors and walls inside. But even now, some fifty years later, I can still remember vividly the smell of newly polished wood, the feel of sitting at wooden desks with ink wells that were never used, and the unnerving oversight provided by the requisite number of crucifixes on the classroom walls.

I had been in Kingsford almost three months by September, but the only person I knew at St. Theresa's was Hannah Austin who lived down the street from Andy. Hannah lived with her mother in a dilapidated wooden house that was badly in need of repair and repainting. The mother had been abandoned by her husband when Hannah was a baby. She was ill. I can't recall the nature of her illness, but one look at her pale, almost translucent skin would convince you that her days were numbered.

Malignant Memory

Andy had brought me to the Austin house specifically to meet Hannah when I first arrived in Kingsford. "She's your age and she goes to St. Theresa's," Andy told me. "She's a little different, but at least you'll know someone when you start school."

The visit had not gone well.

Andy left me alone with Hannah while she ministered to Hannah's ailing mother. Hannah sat on a kitchen chair, reading a book. Unlike her tiny mother, Hannah was stocky in build, with broad shoulders and a square chin. Her mousy brown hair was short, cut in straggly, uneven strands across her head. It looked as if she cut it herself without looking in a mirror. It was an inch shorter than the shortest haircut I had ever seen on a girl.

Hannah was dressed in a man's flannel shirt and brown corduroy pants. She looked like a boy.

"Aren't you hot?" I asked her. It was my attempt to initiate a conversation. "It's ninety-two degrees outside and I am sweltering." Hannah did not look up at me. She did not acknowledge me in any way.

I felt stupid, nervous. I tried again. "Did you see the movie that's playing downtown? The one with Doris Day and Rock Hudson? I hear it's supposed to be wonderful."

Still no response.

"Andy says that I can wear lipstick when I start school." I could not believe I had said that! I sounded like a prattling idiot.

Hannah peered at me over her book. "Are you that dumb? Really?" she asked in her most disdainful tone. "Do you not see that I am reading here? That I have no interest in you or your inane conversation? There are real issues in the world that need my attention. I could care less about movies or makeup. If you don't have anything better to do than to talk about nonsense, I'd like it if you kept quiet while I read my book." She resumed her reading as if I had never existed. I cringed in embarrassment as I waited in silence for Andy to reappear.

Hannah's brashness, her facility to demand what she wanted, both repulsed and fascinated me. If I were honest, I would have to admit that Hannah and I shared an irritation with superficial talk. But Hannah's intensity, her defiance of all things conventional, scared me.

I vowed on that first meeting that I would ignore Hannah at school. Whenever I saw her at school or on the street, I pretended she didn't exist.

An Education

I looked the other way.

I was lonely in my first months at St. Theresa High. I had no friends.

There is a prevailing myth that everyone is the same in Catholic schools, that no one is more privileged than anyone else. It is believed that students wear the same uniforms, and therefore they are all equal. There is an assumption that because Christian values are espoused, every student is treated equally.

It is true that we all wore the same uniforms: a navy jumper, white long-sleeved blouse, thick beige stockings, and lace-up black leather shoes. It is also true that the teachers emphasized being kind to one another, turning the other cheek, and living a life that was Christ-like. But there were other things that highlighted my unacceptable difference within the school.

Most of my classmates had been together in school since the earliest grades. They saw me, a stranger, as an unwanted intruder in their midst. They teased me about my shyness. They laughed at me when I did not know things they had grown up knowing about the town and its people. They made fun of me for coming from a farm, having white blonde hair that would not hold a curl, being taller than most of the girls in my grade, being extraordinarily thin, and living with my grandmother.

The other girls assumed that because I was reserved and shy, I was arrogant. They called me Queen Elizabeth. The nickname was derisive, not a sign of inclusion and camaraderie, as my grandmother had promised. Girls chanted mockingly, "Here comes the queen" as I walked by them in the hallways. They circulated rumours that I was in Kingsford because I had a baby and had to give it up for adoption. They told each other that I was stuck up and ignorant.

My status as a trespasser in the school was cinched one day shortly after I began attending the school. My classmates were sharing jokes about the local pulp mill in the school cafeteria. They referred to Kingsford as Sulphurford and Kings Farts. They giggled that everyone knew they were from Kingsford because even their sweat smelled of sulphur.

The putrid aroma of the mill woke me from a sound sleep at times. It burned my throat. My skin, my hair, and my sheets were drenched in the odour of rotten eggs. I was tempted to join in, to make belittling comments about the mill, but I knew instinctively that while my peers could speak of the mill's odour in disparaging ways, I as an outsider could never make the same jokes. If I was ever going to be embraced as one of them, I needed to keep criticisms about the mill's stink to myself until I had earned the rank of insider.

I quoted Andy's script about the mill. I said, "The smell is only bad some days. And it's a smell of prosperity." The girls stopped their chatter abruptly. One girl, the obvious leader of the group, sneered that I had no right to speak about the mill. She said that I was not a true Kingsfordian. I was from somewhere else. She told me that no one was interested in my thoughts about the mill. Or anything else for that matter. "We have no time for trash like you," she said.

I was astonished by the onslaught of ill will that I received from the other girls. Back home, I had been nurtured and admired in the one-room school. The teacher and my classmates had referred to me as clever and personable. I had no resources to deal with the inexplicable hatred directed toward me.

I was an unwelcome immigrant. I was a displaced person. I did not belong. I slunk into obscurity.

I only spoke when a teacher asked me a direct question about schoolwork; that happened only rarely. I hung my head as I walked down the school halls. I ate alone in the school cafeteria. I approached no one. The only one in my class who was more unpopular than me was Hannah Austin. There was much about Hannah that made her a target for hostility among both the students and the teachers.

Hannah became a raging bull whenever she thought someone was trying to make her do something she did not want to do. She refused to accept teachers' dictates without an explanation that satisfied her. She made fun of students and teachers who were unquestioning about what they did and believed.

Hannah was bright, but her grades were poor. She was not a believer in exams, assignments, or marks. She regularly completed only half a test just to show the teacher that she did not care about such things. Her answers to the test questions she answered were always correct.

Hannah seemed not to care about others' opinions of her. She danced with abandon and sang opera loudly in the hallways of the school. She did this although she had no particular talent and despite the daily reprimands she received from the principal for her "lack of

An Education

decorum". She seemed not to notice that no one spoke to her except to hurl hurtful epithets. Weirdo. Basket case. Fruitcake.

Most people tried to ignore Hannah. They had learned that to engage Hannah in a battle was to risk public humiliation. Her superior intelligence, perspicacity, and sharp tongue made Hannah a formidable adversary. Hannah was fond of pointing out flaws in people's thinking. She made fun of people's peculiarities in ways that left them feeling exposed and vulnerable.

I too tried to ignore Hannah. I didn't want any of my classmates to know that I knew her. I pretended not to hear or see her when Hannah called out to me one day. "Hey country bumpkin, how's it going?" She did not attempt to speak to me again for many weeks after that encounter.

The teachers at St. Theresa's were mostly nuns. I had never seen a nun before coming to Kingsford. The nuns hid their gender in floor-length black dresses with a white collar and a shoulder length veil held in place by a white headpiece. A rosary hung from a leather belt at their waists. A large crucifix hung around their necks.

My classmates were fond of saying that nuns were special because they were married to Jesus. Most understood that to talk back to a nun or to treat her meanly in any way meant that her husband, Jesus, would get revenge for the wrong done to his wife. Only the bravest and most foolish of students risked such retaliation.

I was fascinated by the nuns' choice to forsake marriage to take up a lifetime of sacrifice and commitment to an ethereal man. I stayed awake at night wondering what accounted for their decision to join the convent and whether they had any hair under their veils. I wondered, but dared not question, whether they ever regretted their decision to enter the convent, whether they missed having a real man kiss and hold them.

The nuns were appalled by my ignorance of Catholicism. Many of them remembered my father as a fervent Catholic. I knew Father had attended church with Andy when he lived in Kingsford, but Father had implied this was to please his mother, not because he had any faith. I had no idea that Catholicism had once been important to him. My own family had not attended church. Father had instructed me to say I was Catholic if ever I were asked, but I had little idea of what that meant. One nun told me that I was obviously rebellious if I had chosen to ignore my father's example as a good Catholic.

Malignant Memory

The nuns required me to take additional religion classes to improve my knowledge of Catholicism. I made several critical errors in those classes that solidified my reputation among the nuns that I was without promise of redemption.

I asked Sister Joseph if it was true that some of the Popes had fathered children. She spluttered and then assigned me detention. I questioned Sister Martha about why a loving God would send unbaptized babies to Purgatory—a waiting room for those who weren't bad enough to be assigned to hell but not good enough for heaven. I had to write "I will not question my faith" a thousand times before she said Jesus forgave me. I learned quickly that my curiosity about Catholicism was regarded as insolence. My questions were not welcome.

Most of the nuns were nice enough. Some were good teachers. But they were stern. They discouraged displays of enjoyment and hilarity. They emphasized the importance of discipline and self-control. Laughing and having fun, even in the school cafeteria, were thought to be markers of poor moral fibre.

It's a law of averages that there has to be a requisite number of ugly-hearted people in any group. There were some mean teachers at St. Theresa's. Watching how these vicious teachers intentionally humiliated students was my first life lesson in the evil that is inherent in the abuse of power. I cringed when Mrs. Leblanc who taught Latin refused to allow Betty Porter to leave the class to go to the bathroom. She gave no reason for her decision. She merely said, "No. Sit down." A trail of yellow urine escaped down Betty's leg. It trickled on the floor toward the back of the room. Some of the students made disgusted noises. They snickered. Betty sat at her desk in her pee-soaked underwear, tears streaming down her cheeks, until the class was dismissed an hour later.

The teachers who were cruel and spiteful tended to leave me alone. They did not notice me. I imagine they had no reason to see me. My marks were good. I obeyed the rules. I was quiet. I did not challenge them. I was invisible.

Sister Agnes, the principal, was the epitome of mean at St. Theresa's. Sister Agnes was a short, wizened nun who seemed decades older than the other teachers. She marched down the corridors, long metal ruler in hand, ready to pounce on any student who was

An Education

disregarding one of the school's many rules. Chewing gum, forgetting to remove winter boots at the door, and talking after the bell had rung were just a few of the offences worthy of corporal punishment.

Sister Agnes had an uncanny knack for seeing things that she was not meant to see. She could detect even the slightest of violations with few cues. A small scurry in the hallway, a student seeming unusually nonchalant, or someone avoiding looking at her was enough for her to determine that an offence had been committed.

Sister Agnes delivered her punishments swiftly. The offender was not given an opportunity to defend herself. Sister Agnes would tell the girl to raise her hand to chest level, palm upwards. Then she would strike the girl's palm with her ruler. Whack! Whack! She struck with vengeance, as if her entire purpose in life was to beat out the girl's wickedness. The sound of ruler hitting skin could be heard several classrooms away.

The number of slaps a student received was determined solely by Sister Agnes. She told us on the first day of school that she had a system to figure out how many slaps of the ruler were justified by an offence. Being late for class warranted eight slaps. Talking back to a teacher was reason for 15 slaps.

Sister Agnes did not apply her system consistently.

Hannah Austin was two minutes late to class one morning. Sister Agnes cornered Hannah in the hallway. Sister Agnes held up her ruler victoriously. She looked delighted at having caught Hannah in her crime. She began beating Hannah's palms. Hannah smiled broadly as if she were enjoying herself, as if the beatings were pleasurable. The veins in Sister Agnes' neck throbbed. Her face turned blotchy red. Her eyes flashed with fury. Her rage grew. It overtook her.

Hannah received 55 slaps of the ruler, not eight. Hannah's palms were bleeding at the end of the beating. Hannah was smiling, grinning widely from ear to ear at the end of the assault. Sister Agnes was winded, exhausted.

I was horrified that a teacher could treat a student in that way. But I thought Hannah had contributed to her punishment by refusing to be contrite. She's bad news, I thought to myself. I strengthened my resolve to stay away from Hannah.

Sister Agnes only hit me once. She thought I was late for class.

Malignant Memory

She was wrong. A teacher had asked me to go to the office for a stapler. I tried to tell Sister Agnes that I was not late, but she would not listen. Sister Agnes hit me hard, eight times. My hand burned where the ruler had made its crimson stains. Other students crowded around us to watch me receiving my punishment. Some looked horrified. A few looked away, embarrassed to be a witness to my humiliation. Others grinned as if the beating was my just desserts.

Hannah was there, watching. She smiled at me. I was surprised by the gentleness of her smile.

Sister Agnes told me she had hit me to make me a better person in the sight of God. She ordered me to thank her for what she had done. I knew if I did not say these things that Sister Agnes' retribution would be swift and painful. I said what she demanded I say. The words were bitter, like vinegar, coming out of my mouth.

The nuns told us that we were lucky to be girls. The boys in the boys' school were disciplined by the priests by being hit over their face, heads and necks. One nun explained, "Sister Agnes would never hit a girl on her face because a girl's face is her treasure. If a girl isn't going to the convent to become a nun, it's important for her to have a beautiful face. It affects her marriage prospects, her success in her career, everything important. With boys, it doesn't really matter how they look."

I stared at my reflection in the mirror each morning, hoping that through some mysterious metamorphosis I had become beautiful overnight. The gaunt, bird-like features of my father and my grandmother looked back at me. I knew was doomed to an unexceptional life because of my unremarkable appearance.

I was miserable at St. Theresa's. I had no friends. I walked to and from school by myself. I was never invited to anyone's house. I thought I had never been so unhappy.

I was unprepared for how grim life would become.

CHAPTER FOUR

THE BEAST

The weather became suddenly cooler. The fall leaves began to drop in earnest. It happened late one Saturday afternoon. I was in my bedroom reading. I could hear Andy banging pots and dishes in the kitchen. She had said nothing to me for three hours. It was a welcome reprieve from her constant chatter. I thought she was being considerate, giving me space to read quietly on my own. Andy yelled to me from the kitchen, "Come get supper."

Supper was tasteless. The chicken was stringy. The creamed corn and overcooked chicken combination looked like pale vomit on the plate. Andy did not talk.

I made several feeble attempts to initiate conversation.

"Who taught you how to cook?"

Silence.

"I like these dishes. They are pretty. Have you had them a long time?"

No response.

Andy turned to stare at me. She looked at me as if I had suddenly materialized in her kitchen. She seemed to be looking through me, as if I had no actual substance. I felt uncomfortable, suddenly afraid of what was to come.

I ate quickly, forcing myself to swallow. I took my dishes to the sink and started to fill the sink with water.

Andy rose from her chair so hastily that the chair toppled, making a loud crashing sound as it landed on the tile floor. It startled me. I turned to see what had happened.

Malignant Memory

I was unprepared for her slap across my cheek. "You worthless, ungrateful brat," she screamed as she flailed her fists, striking me repeatedly around my head. "You didn't even say grace before your meal. You didn't thank the Lord. You didn't thank me. You have no manners. You're worse than a child in the gutters. I can't stand the sight of you. Get out of here before I kill you."

She continued to hammer me with blows across my face, chest and arms for several minutes. Even as she beat me, she did not seem to see me. Her eyes were glazed, her face contorted with hate.

I had never been more terrified. It had happened so quickly. I could not understand why she had struck me, why she had said the things she did. My cheeks and chest burned where her hands had made contact with my skin. The collision of her gold wedding band on my cheekbone left a throbbing pain below my left eye.

Andy paused for a second, breathless. I fled to my bedroom. I was petrified that Andy would pursue me. I positioned the cot as a barrier by the closed door. I heard her muttering to herself in the kitchen, still professing my sins but calmer now and not screaming.

I was overcome with loneliness and fear. I curled my body in a fetal position on the cot, hugging the doll, Betsy. I wept until sleep provided a longed-for escape.

Early the next morning, I heard Andy singing in the kitchen. "Don't sit under the apple tree with anyone else but me, anyone else but me." She sang noisily. I had never heard her sing outside of church.

I glanced at my reflection in the pocket mirror I had brought from home. Bruises were beginning to form on my cheeks, chest, and forearms. I ached everywhere.

Andy knocked gently on the bedroom door. "Elizabeth," she called to me sweetly, "I have made you breakfast. Let's have breakfast together and we will plan our day."

I looked vainly around the room for an escape. I tried not answering her, but she persisted. Finally, I said, "I'll be there as soon as I brush my teeth."

"All right. I will be waiting for you whenever you are ready." I escaped into the bathroom. I sat on the toilet, planning how I would face her. Should I confront her with what she had done? Should I tell a neighbour? Should I demand to be sent home? Should I pretend that it hadn't happened? Should I write to my parents and tell them?

I sat on the toilet for a long time, posing possible reactions to my dilemma. None of the responses I proposed seemed realistic. I was sure that none of the neighbours who adored Andy would believe she had done such a thing. Confronting Andy would undoubtedly lead to more manifestations of her anger. My parents could not afford the train fare to send me home.

I went into the kitchen for breakfast, acutely aware of Andy staring at me. She smiled at me fondly when I sat at the table. I winced as she moved her hand to touch my cheek. "Oh, poor you," she said. "You have bruises from that fall you had yesterday. I'll put ice on them, that'll make them feel better. For now, I think you should rest. I have some books about the saints I think you might like to read. I'll make you some lemonade. You can just rest and get better."

What fall? Is she crazy? I had not fallen. Was it possible she did not remember what she had done?

The breakfast was delicious. Andy had bought cinnamon buns from the bakery down the street. She had squeezed oranges to make juice. She was kind, attentive, and motherly. I began to think that I had imagined the whole thing—the assault had never happened.

Later in my bedroom, I stared at my face in the pocket mirror. I touched my badly bruised cheekbone. I felt the spongy, swollen areas where she had hit my face and chest with her fists. Andy's rage and its expression had been real. But she seemed so contrite, even if she had not explicitly said what had happened or that she felt sorry for what she had done. I decided to act as if it hadn't happened.

Neither of us acknowledged the incident in the days to come. I was aloof and vigilant initially, but gradually, when no further attack occurred, I resumed my usual ways and routines.

For three weeks, Andy was kinder, more attentive and more solicitous than ever before. I was lulled into a false sense of security and calm.

One afternoon, I returned from school. I left my books on the kitchen table while I went to retrieve the mail from the mailbox. I had received a letter from home. I sat down on the edge of the cot to read it.

Andy met me in my bedroom. She began to hit me, to punch

and slap me, screaming that I was messy and inconsiderate. "You wretched girl," she yelled in my ear. "You just don't care about anyone but you. You leave your things anywhere you please. You never think of me." She pinned me with her body against the roll-top desk. I ducked from her blows as much as I could, but I could not escape.

Just like before, she emitted a steady stream of grievances against me, derogating my personality, looks, intelligence, and behaviour. She did not appear to see me as she struck me. She did not call me by name. She continued to strike until she was exhausted by the effort. She retreated to her bedroom, leaving me to weep uncontrollably on my cot.

Just as before, Andy did not acknowledge the attack the morning after. She implied that the bruises and marks left by her blows were due to me playing basketball in the school gymnasium. "You have to learn not to be so aggressive when you are playing sports. Look what you have done to your poor face."

Andy sent a note to the gym teacher asking that she watch over me because I tended to bruise. She implied I had a bleeding disorder. She wrote, "Elizabeth just gets too enthusiastic when she plays. She doesn't watch out for her poor body. She knows she has to be extra cautious, but she forgets to be careful." The gym teacher read the note. She glanced up at me, puzzled. She shrugged. "I didn't see you get hurt. I'll pay better attention."

The gym teacher was very fond of Andy. Andy babysat for her so that she and her husband could attend bingo every week.

No one at school seemed to notice my injuries. Hannah Austin had stopped me in the hallway once. "What's going on?" she demanded to know. "I see your bruises. I know someone is doing this to you. Who did it?" I pushed by her. I did not answer. She did not pursue me.

Just as before, Andy was tender and loving for a time after the attack. But this time, for many days afterward, I avoided contact with Andy. I stayed in my bedroom for long hours. I said I wasn't hungry when she called me for a meal. It took much longer for us to resume our usual life.

The pattern of attack, followed by a period of calm and solicitous attention, was repeated over and over in my first six months in Kingsford. Once, the time between attacks was more than four weeks. Another time, the attacks were less than a week apart.

The Beast

I reasoned that if I avoided all the things that made her angry, Andy would not hit me. I made a catalogue in my journal of what I could remember she had screamed during the attacks about the provocation for the assaults. I listed the following as harbingers of her rage:
1. Me not saying hello when I come home from school
2. Me leaving my books in the kitchen
3. Me not thanking her for what she did
4. Me leaving the radio on when I went to school
5. Me not cleaning the bathtub after I used it
6. Me being too loud
7. Me being too quiet
8. Me being clumsy or dropping things
9. Me forgetting to say grace before meals
10. Me forgetting to tell her some news from the neighbours
11. Me forgetting to say "Good morning" or "Good night" to her
12. Me forgetting to do almost anything
13. Me being later than I said
14. Me being earlier than I said

I used the list as the map of how I should behave around Andy. I became methodical about saying grace, expressing gratitude, cleaning the bathtub, switching off the radio when I left the house, and putting my school books in my bedroom. I also worked at coming home exactly when I said I would. Sometimes this meant staying several minutes at the park at the end of Andy's street so I wouldn't appear earlier than I had said I would.

It didn't stop the attacks.

Sometimes Andy yelled that I was being too loud when she hit me. Other times, she said I was being too quiet. It seemed to me that I was the same on these occasions. I could not discern the difference. I tried not to drop things, but when I accidentally spilled milk, it was the impetus for her to beat me. Sister Agatha asked me to stay after class to discuss my joining the debate team. The extra 10 minutes meant I was later than usual coming home from school. Andy's attack was fierce and prolonged.

The provocations for Andy's assaults expanded almost weekly. Soon I could no longer anticipate what might be the precursor to her rages. Sometimes during an attack, she screamed things to me that I

Malignant Memory

had not done. Once she said, "You were supposed to watch over the little girls and you didn't. Now one of them is hurt." I had no idea what she meant.

I became nervous and jittery around Andy, unsure if I would do something to provoke another of her "fits." I decided that if I could detect the signs of an imminent attack, I could run for shelter before the assault began. I wrote down a list of signs that an attack was imminent:

1. Her banging pots or dishes
2. Her avoiding looking at me
3. Her being unusually quiet
4. Her cheek muscles twitching
5. Her drinking from her "medicine" bottle that she kept hidden under the kitchen sink
6. Her going to bed in the afternoon
7. Her not eating the food on her plate
8. Her staring out the kitchen window
9. Her using profanity
10. Her using the Lord's name in vain

I would see the tell-tale signs—slamming pots and a twitching cheek muscle were ominous portents—and I would run to my bedroom for shelter. This was often sufficient to protect me from getting hit. I would hear Andy yelling in another room, but I was safe. Other times, Andy forced her way into my bedroom. I could not escape her fists as they did their damage to my body and my person.

After the mood passed, Andy would try to make up for what had occurred by being extra nice, but the wake of her tempest was felt for many days. I trod carefully around her, afraid to rouse another storm.

I prayed to the God I had only recently been introduced to. I begged Him to make her stop, to tell me how to be good so that she wouldn't hit me, to make her pay for the hurt she had caused me, to warn my parents so that they would return me to the farm. God ignored my prayers.

The neighbours and my teachers seemed not to see the blackened eyes, the welts on the cheeks, the bruises on my arms and face. Mr. Clarke, the baker, once said to Andy, "She sure seems to fall a lot." Andy agreed that I was clumsy. "I don't know what to do with her. Her parents warned me she has two left feet."

The Beast

I can't understand, even now after all these years, why I didn't yell at her to stop. Why I didn't fight back. I was not a reticent child. On the farm, I could wallop my brothers, even the older ones, if I thought they deserved it. Perhaps I thought if I did anything to stop Andy during one of her "fits," her wrath would be even greater and more prolonged. Or perhaps I was just too paralyzed to think about anything but retreat. I know that as the attacks continued, I began to think that I was somehow deserving of Andy's beatings. I gradually saw myself through her words as inept, insensitive, and ungrateful. I began to believe that perhaps Andy had no choice but to beat the evil out of me.

Andy commanded me to stay away from school after a particularly brutal attack. She claimed that a recent outbreak of chicken pox made it too dangerous for me to attend school. She left the house to attend to a neighbour.

I walked gingerly to the church, my entire body aching, my thoughts muddled and anxious. I told Father McKenzie in the confessional, "She beats me—for no reason. I am scared she's going to kill me." I offered to show him my bruises, the welts across my face and arms, my black eye. Father McKenzie answered that my grandmother knew what was best for me, that I needed her discipline. He had heard about my impudence in the religion classes at school. He was grateful to Andy for all the work she did to help others in the community. She bought him fresh buns from the bakery every Monday.

Father McKenzie assigned me penance. "Five Hail Mary's and ten Our Father's." He told me to thank God for what Andy was doing for me. "Andy is a good Christian woman. You are lucky to have her as a grandmother."

I walked home, miserable and defeated. The park by Andy's house stood deserted and bleak in the fading snow. I sat on one of the swings, dejected, shivering from the cold. I did not want to go back to Andy's house. I knew I could not go home to the farm. There was no money for the train fare. It was too far to walk. No one seemed to care that Andy was hitting me.

I was stuck in the torrent of Andy's unpredictable fury.

I began to cry. Tears flowed down my cheeks, soaking the collar of my cloth coat.

Malignant Memory

"Hi there," a woman's voice called. It was a kind and gentle voice. It promised compassion, nurture. I looked up from my downcast view of the ground beneath the swing.

It was a tiny bird of a woman. She was sitting in a wheelchair. Although it was clear that she was an adult, everything about her was miniature. Even her wheelchair was diminutive.

It was difficult to judge her age. She was small, about the size of a five-year-old, but there were a few wisps of grey in her dark brown hair. Her face was elfin, pretty in a fairy-like way. Her wrists were half the size of my own. Her tiny legs were twisted beneath her, in a scissor-like fashion. Her chest was barrelled, wider than her shoulders, resting in her lap, concealing her breasts.

"Hi, I'm Margaret Foster," she said. "People call me 'Brain'. We haven't met. How do you do?" Then she stuck out her hand.

I walked hesitantly to the sidewalk to greet her. The tiny woman looked directly me. Her pale blue eyes were full of such tenderness that I began to sob with relief. I had found someone who would help me.

The woman called Brain reached up from her chair to hug my shoulders. I hung onto her as if I were drowning, and she was my lifejacket.

Brain was to prove to be my saviour in the coming months. Not only did she help me to live with Andy in peace, but she became my true friend. Meeting her was the beginning of fulfillment and happiness in Kingsford.

It was also a prologue to the nightmare; the secret I have guarded all these years.

CHAPTER FIVE

BRAIN AND CRANE

Margaret asked me to call her by the name given to her by the people of Kingsford. "Please call me Brain. Everyone else does. They call me that because they think I am smart. I won some awards in high school. After that, I was Brain. This town loves to give people nicknames." She laughed delightedly.

She gave a small snort as she said, laughing, "My husband is Crane. His real name is William. The people in town call him Crane because he's very strong. He lifts me and the chair up and down stairs, and pretty well everywhere we need to go. Crazy huh? Brain and Crane? I call him Crane, and he calls me Brain. We are so used to it. We almost never use our real names anymore."

Brain motioned for me to join her, as she wended her way down the slippery sidewalk.

"I am meeting Crane here in a few minutes. He doesn't like it when I am on my own outside. The sidewalk is uneven. It has icy patches. He worries I will fall out of my chair. I told him I just needed a little time to myself. He'll be waiting for me at the exit from the park, shortly. Maybe we can get to know one another a bit while I wait."

We walked along the sidewalk, her in her wheelchair and me beside her. She asked me questions about where I lived, how long I had lived in Kingsford, what I liked to do. I told her that I had come from the farm to be with Andy. Brain said she had known Andy all her life. I could not make out if Brain liked Andy. She merely said that she knew her.

Malignant Memory

I told Brain that I loved reading above everything else. She said that reading was her favourite pastime as well. She asked me what books were my favourites.

I explained that my access to books at the farm had been limited. The only library back home was in the one-room school and consisted of two wooden shelves. The books had been donated through a bequest by a university professor, a philosopher, who had retired to our community. Most of the books were too adult for young readers such as myself to comprehend, but as I loved reading and these were the only books available to me, I read each one—sometimes several times over. The books not only improved my vocabulary, they also expanded my horizons beyond our small farming community. In the words of the authors, I could escape my life on the farm to fantasize of someday being a famous orator, delivering weighty treatises about life to audiences who were in awe of my genius and eloquence.

My favourite book among the one-room school's collection was Plato's Apology. I was particularly fond of Plato's account of the trial of Socrates. On days when one of my brothers' pranks went awry and I was held to blame, I read about the courage of the much-maligned Socrates and felt vindicated. I admitted somewhat sheepishly to Brain that I often lay on my bed and imagined authors writing after my death about how my parents had wronged me for blaming me for pranks committed by my brothers. Once, I tried to find hemlock on our farm so that I could join Socrates in his fate as an inspired but misunderstood thinker.

Brain laughed delightedly, "I love that book too. Did you read any novels in school? Books about travel? Nature?"

I shook my head. Other than the philosophy books, we had a few excerpts of books to read, the Reader's Digest version of literature, but no others. The reading we did in the one-room school was confined to our textbooks.

Brain said, "I am the librarian in the local library. I'd love to show you the library any time you like. I will introduce you to some books that will change your world."

Her voice was gentle, her manner so open and affirming, that I found myself telling her about the farm. I described my brothers' antics. I told her how I came to Kingsford. Why I lived with Andy. I told her about how lonely I was, how much I missed my family. I told her that I hated my school, that my classmates were mean, and that I did not understand much of Catholicism.

I told her, "I like the church services, the Masses. They're comforting, peaceful. I like the statues in the chapel. You can relate to the stories of the saints better when you have an image of them in your mind. Some of them look so kind, as if they would be your best friend if they were alive. But I have so many questions about being a Catholic. The nuns don't like my questions, but I still have them. Like they say that the Pope is infallible; he never makes mistakes. How can that be? Lots of Popes have made mistakes. And why are they all men? I get into trouble with the nuns when I ask these questions. They say I am being impudent and rude. I don't know why. I really want to know the answers to my questions."

Brain chortled, "They take questions about what they believe rather personally, don't they?" she asked sardonically. "I had the same problem when I went to a public school. The teachers there wanted to be taken at face value. I couldn't do it. I had to understand before I believed."

I told Brain that my nickname at school was Queen Elizabeth. Brain replied, "That's good. Around here, to have a nickname means they accept you. You're one of them."

I answered that the reference to royalty was not a positive one. I described how the kids at school made exaggerated bowing gestures to me as I walked down the school corridors. How they sneered my nickname when a teacher announced that I had the top marks in an exam. Brain thought for a moment.

"They only call you this in school, right?"

I nodded.

She spoke animatedly, grinning widely.

"I know what we'll do. We will start calling you something else. We'll make sure it catches on. Once the people in Kingsford know you as that, the other name won't have a foothold. It'll disappear.

"So what shall we call you? How about Lizzie? No, that won't do. Too ordinary. We need something that makes you unique, interesting—something that tells your story so people want to know more.

"It's too bad that your classmates have made fun of Elizabeth. I love the name Elizabeth. Someday, I'll introduce you to Elizabeth

Malignant Memory

Bennett in Jane Austen's Pride and Prejudice. Now there's a model of a woman, that Elizabeth Bennett."

Brain provided a rapid succession of nicknames for me to consider. She crossed these off her list as soon as she spoke them. Some she declared as too provincial. Others she declined because she thought they did not do me justice.

"Your last name is Anderson. We could call you Andy2. No, we don't want people thinking you are a second Andy. I like her, but I think you are your own person, right?"

I nodded.

"Professor? They will all know how smart you are. No, that might cause your classmates to resent you even more than they do now."

Brain stopped her wheelchair and looked into the distance.

After what seemed a long time, she said, "Never mind. We'll think of something. You just leave it with me."

We walked for several minutes, both of us lost in our thoughts. Suddenly, without warning, Brain asked, "Do you want to tell me about that black eye?"

It was then that I decided to tell her my secret. I hesitated, afraid that she wouldn't believe me, or worse, that she would blame me. I blurted, "She hits me sometimes, my grandmother. I try to be good, but it doesn't help. She keeps on hitting me until she's tired and she has to stop. She's nice afterward, but she never says she's sorry. She pretends it never happened. And then it happens again. Maybe in a few days, or a week, but it happens again. I don't know how to make her stop hitting me."

I paused to judge her response. She was looking at me with such compassion that I started to weep huge, heaving sobs. I managed to say, "She didn't want me to go to school today. She's afraid that someone will see my black eye. I went to confession today to talk to Father McKenzie about it."

"Yes? What did he say?"

"He said Andy needed to do it. It was my fault."

"Stupid fucking idiot." I was startled by her profanity and the intensity of her anger. "What does he know about real life, a priest whose only real relationship is with his dog? Obviously this is not your fault. Your grandmother should not be hitting you."

Brain and Crane

I had never heard anyone refer to a priest in such an irreverent way. I looked nervously at the ground, certain that we were about to be swallowed whole by a cavern in the earth.

In a few seconds, I no longer cared about how Brain had spoken about the priest. I was flooded with relief. I was believed.

Brain said, "Crane will be waiting. We should get a move on. Come with me." It was a command but she said it gently, as if it were an invitation.

Brain motioned for me to push her wheelchair. She relaxed in the chair as I pushed, holding my hand as we walked. She said nothing more about my black eye or about what I had told her.

Crane was waiting for us. He was leaning against a light post, reading a book. I glanced at the book and read the title, Being and Time. I recognized it from the philosophy collection in my one-room school back home. I had found the book almost incomprehensible. I wondered briefly if Crane would be willing to help me understand it. Crane was short. I was taller than him by a few inches. He was not a handsome man. His features were too rugged to be considered attractive. His cheekbones were pronounced. His nose was broad, flattened. A small scar lay across the bridge of his nose. Another one marked the right side of his forehead. There was a wide shock of white along the crown of his head, accenting the darkness of his ebony hair.

A wayward curl kept falling over Crane's left eye as he read. He distractedly waved the hair from his view and looked up to face us. His deep brown eyes conveyed kindness, gentleness.

Crane bent down to kiss Brain on the lips. They lingered in that pose. I looked away, embarrassed by the raw demonstration of love I was witnessing.

"This is Elizabeth," Brain told him. "She's my new friend. We're going to walk her to Andy's house. Andy is her grandmother. She's staying with Andy for three years."

Crane doffed his cap brim in my direction, bowing slightly as if before royalty. "Pleased to meet you, new friend."

Crane positioned himself behind Brain's wheelchair. He began to propel her down the street. Brain and I continued to talk. She asked me about who I knew in Kingsford. What my grandmother had told me about the town. I told her about our cemetery visits and the stories Andy would tell there.

Malignant Memory

Brain said, "You are a reader and a lover of stories. You say you have no friends, but soon I will introduce you to new friends. They are in books. They will become lifelong friends. They will be with you even when it seems as if everybody living has deserted you."

Brain told me then about how she fell in love with Crane. She said that she was not expected to live when she was born. She never walked on her own. As a child, she had frequent bouts of pneumonia, each threatening to end her life. She was an only child. Her parents doted on her. "They treated me as if I might break any minute. They loved me, but they suffocated me. They were afraid to let me do anything on my own. They fought me about anything I wanted to do if it meant even the tiniest risk."

Brain said that she wanted to experience as much of life as she could, even at an early age. "What I lack in size and stamina, I make up for in stubbornness and perseverance."

Crane was her classmate. They had attended the same school since grade three.

Brain had the highest marks in her high school graduating class. The person with the highest marks was always chosen to be the valedictorian at the graduation exercises. Shortly before graduation, the principal announced that Crane, not her, would be giving the valedictory address.

Brain confronted the principal. She pointed out that she had higher marks than Crane. The principal responded, "You should be grateful that we even allowed you to be a student here. Most people in your circumstances can't think about going to high school."

The principal said that the school would have to arrange alterations to the convocation podium if she were to give the valedictory address. "The audience could never see you if you sat on the stage in your wheelchair." He told her that the complexity of the renovations and having to arrange someone to carry Brain up and down the stairs to the stage were too taxing to consider. Crane was the best option as valedictorian.

There was thinly disguised fury in Brain's voice when she related her conversation with the principal. "He was embarrassed that the valedictorian would be in a wheelchair, not standing on her own behind the podium. People in wheelchairs were pretty much invisible, back then in the forties. And that's the way they preferred us. We made some people feel uncomfortable because we weren't 'normal.'"

Brain and Crane

Brain looked up at Crane, standing behind her, and smiled at him. "Crane knew I had better marks than he did. We had been in the same class since we were eight years old, but I hadn't thought much about him. He was quiet. Never talked. He was smart, but he seemed so aloof. Anyway, when Crane heard I wasn't going to be the valedictorian, he got the whole graduating class to sign a petition. The principal tried to ignore the petition.

"Crane was relentless in his campaign to make me valedictorian. He wrote letters to the principal, to the school board, to the local paper. He contacted each of the parents of the kids in our class. The parents of our classmates started phoning the principal, demanding that he respond to the petition. The principal had to make me valedictorian.

"I asked Crane why he had done what he had done. He told me, 'I think you are amazing, the smartest and most beautiful woman I have ever met. I will do anything in my power to help you be who you are meant to be, to make the world see what I see.' Who wouldn't fall in love with someone like that?

"Turned out that he had been in love with me for years—ever since he saw me in my wheelchair on the ice on the lake, skating with the other kids. He said I was so full of life that he just fell head over heels in love.

"After high school, I applied to university in Toronto. I wanted to be a librarian. The university denied my application because the building had stairs, no elevators. Crane made an appointment with the Dean to say that he promised to carry me up and down the four flights of stairs for the entire length of my program. He was true to his promise. I graduated with honours. We got married six months later.

"I applied to be a librarian here in Kingsford. The municipality rejected my application. They said there were stairs in the library. They thought I couldn't manage them. Crane convinced them that if I got the job, he would carry me up and down the stairs whenever I needed help. I have been working there twenty-three years now. I love it. And I love that Crane shares the library with me."

Brain paused. "You know, sometimes people look at me and they feel sorry for me. They think that it's sad that I can't walk, that I have to rely on someone else, my husband, just to get around. But I see

Malignant Memory

it differently. Crane and I are best friends, closer than most people who are married. We share our lives in a real way every day."

Crane bent down over the back of the wheelchair to kiss her on the top of her head.

We came to a curb at an intersection of the road. Crane picked up Brain in her chair as easily as I handled my hairbrush. He lifted her to the height of his shoulders. He kissed her on her forehead. He placed her and her chair gently on the pavement. Brain looked up at him from her chair and smiled.

Brain motioned for us to stop. She patted the seat of a bench at a bus stop. "Sit," she said to me. I sat down and waited.

"I am going to tell you about Andy, at least what I know about Andy. I think it may help you. You see, Andy and my Aunt Thelma are good friends. When I was little, my mother got TB and had to go away to a sanatorium. My father asked his oldest brother, my uncle Frank, to look after me. Frank was married to Thelma. Thelma's Cree, an Indian. Thelma lives near the reserve, not on the reserve like Thelma's brothers and sisters. She lost her status as an Indian when she married a white man, so she can't live on the reserve."

"I have never heard about Thelma," I interrupted.

"Andy and Thelma used to see each other every day, but now Thelma has bad legs. She doesn't leave the house much because of the pain. And neither Thelma nor Andy can drive a car. Thelma lives too far away for Andy to walk to her house. Neither of them likes the telephone."

Brain paused, "I guess they are foul weather friends now. They seem to see each other only when things are very bad for one of them. But when they get together, it's as if they have never been apart."

She continued her story as if there had been no interruption.

"So I was to go to Frank and Thelma's. I was happy to go. My cousins were good to me. Thelma was a wonderful, loving aunt. But one day when Thelma and I were alone together, she started hitting me. She was screaming at me, saying horrible things about me. I thought she hated me. I ran to the woodshed. I was crying. Uncle Frank found me. I told him what happened. He said, 'Ah. It's the furies.' I didn't know what he was talking about.

"Later, one of my cousins told me that Thelma had fits of anger, the "furies," because she had been in a residential school."

"What's a residential school?" I interrupted again.

"I know it's not in your history books—the ones you read in school. But it's a real part of our history. And not one we should be proud of." Brain's face contorted in anger.

"The damn government thought that being an Indian was bad. They thought they had to get rid of the Indian in every Indian child. They took the children away from their families.

"The government built schools, residential schools, where Indian children had to stay to get the Indian out of them. When Thelma was six, she had been playing outside her house with her friends. An Indian agent came to take her to the residential school. He didn't even tell her mother he was taking her. Thelma's mother looked everywhere for Thelma. She thought she'd drowned in the river. The agent took Thelma to a residential school many miles away from her home.

"The staff at the residential school didn't allow the kids to speak their own language. They shaved off their long beautiful braids. The nuns who ran Thelma's school strapped the children for minor offences, like not having their bedcovers straight. If they wet their beds at night, they had to parade in front of the other children, wearing stinky wet sheets on their heads. And then there were other really horrible things. Thelma told me that a nun used to scrub her private parts with a wire brush. The nun thought that would stop Thelma from thinking about sex."

I gasped, appalled.

"Thelma went home for the Christmas break after she had been at the school for a few months. She told her family about the terrible things she had experienced. Her family wouldn't let her go back to the school. The Indian agent came with the Mounties. They forced Thelma's family to give her up. They took her back to the school. The school wouldn't let her go home for holidays after that. They punished Thelma and her family because they hadn't returned Thelma when they were supposed to. She didn't see her family again until she was seventeen. She had forgotten her language by then. She had been taught in residential school that the traditions of her people were bad, that her grandparents and parents were heathens because they were not Christians. She felt she no longer belonged in her own family."

"That's horrible!" I was aghast.

Malignant Memory

Brain nodded in agreement. "I met Andy when I was a teenager. Her husband and Thelma's husband had been friends since childhood. Andy and Thelma would sit by the wood stove and reminisce for hours. They told stories to each other. They let me sit on the floor, listening. They told many of the same kind of stories.

"You see, Thelma went to a residential school and Andy went to an orphanage. Andy and Thelma had some of the same experiences. Both of them experienced things that give me nightmares just thinking about them."

Brain stopped. A man had joined us on the bench. Brain smiled at the man. He nodded. We sat in silence until he boarded a bus and left.

Brain began again. "I remember one story that Thelma told me that made me cry for weeks. She said that her little sister had come to the same residential school. Thelma was thrilled to see her, but the nuns wouldn't let Thelma talk to her. Thelma and her little sister found ways of being together when the nuns weren't looking.

"All the girls slept in a huge room, a dormitory. They slept in metal beds, lined up in a row. One night, the little sister became ill. Thelma knew she was burning up with fever. She begged the nun to take her little sister to the infirmary. The nun told Thelma to mind her own business. The next morning, the little sister was dead. The nuns discovered Thelma in her sister's bed, holding the cold body in her arms. She had climbed into her sister's bed during the night to comfort her. That was against the rules.

"A nun took Thelma to be punished by the priest. He made Thelma take off all her clothes and forced her to lie across his lap. He hit her bare bum over and over with a leather strap until she bled. When she came back to the dormitory, her sister's body had been taken away. The nuns would not allow her to speak of her sister ever again. There was no funeral, no acknowledgement of her death at all."

I sat on the bench, absorbing the horror of what Brain had told me. Finally, I managed to say, "Did Andy experience those things?"

"Things like that—despicable, devastating things. Andy didn't lose her language. She wasn't made to feel stupid and inferior, like Thelma was because she was Indian. But Andy was treated horribly at times. Just like Thelma, she couldn't be a little girl like other little girls. She had to put away her dreams."

Brain pulled a handkerchief out of her jacket pocket. She dabbed at the wetness that had gathered in both eyes.

"Both Andy and Thelma have shattered hearts because of what they experienced. That's why the rage overcomes them sometimes. We call it their 'furies'. Thelma told me once that she hates herself after the furies. She said that during the furies, she does some of the same things that were done to her in the residential school."

Brain paused. "I am going to teach you what my cousins taught me about the furies. The thing is, Thelma and Andy don't really see you when the furies overtake them. It's hard not to take it personally, especially when they are saying terrible things about you, but it isn't personal.

"My cousins told me to think of my aunt as Thelma A and Thelma B. Thelma A is loving, kind, and fun. Thelma B is a ferocious, evil monster who lives inside of Thelma A. What you have to do when the furies strike is to get Thelma A to take over Thelma B. You need to do something that makes Thelma B aware that she has no power over you.

"My cousins told me that the best thing to do is to put some barrier between you and Thelma B. Uncle Frank only smoked when Thelma had the furies. He would light a cigarette and put it in his mouth. It was a signal for Thelma B to back down.

"The other thing my cousins said was to scream at the top of your lungs, 'No!' They said it was enough sometimes to force Thelma A to come to the surface. I tried it and sure enough, it stopped Thelma B in her tracks. You really have to scream though."

"Does your aunt still get the furies?" I asked.

"Less all the time, and not for a long time now. She is working very hard to deal with what happened to her. She is talking to us, her family, about what she experienced so that she can heal. Sometimes she meets with an Elder on the reserve. She is relearning her Cree language. She practices some of the Cree traditions. She has worked really hard to get over what they taught her in residential school—that everything that is Indian is bad. She has found herself again as an Indian woman. She hasn't had the furies for months."

"But Andy doesn't even admit she has the furies. I don't think she wants to stop," I interjected.

"Andy used to have the furies all the time. Your father grew up with those furies. He and your grandfather lived with them. It was hard for them. But Andy hasn't had the furies for a long time. I thought they were gone. What you described to me tells me that the furies are back.

"One thing I know is that when you start to see the furies after they have disappeared for weeks, there's got to be a trigger, something that has made her feel vulnerable and afraid. I am going to introduce you to my Aunt Thelma. Thelma understands Andy. She will find out what the trigger is for Andy's furies."

I felt cold. I could not express my fear. Was I the trigger for Andy's furies?

Brain motioned for us to begin walking again. I struggled to make sense of the cornucopia of emotions I was feeling after Brain's revelation. I was exhausted, hopeful, angry, puzzled, relieved, and overwhelmed with sadness.

We walked together down the sidewalks of Kingsford. Brain asked questions. I answered. Crane listened.

"That's our house," Brain shouted suddenly, pointing across the street from where we stood. The house was similar to the other wartime houses that lined the street. It was small with a steeply pitched roof, small sash windows, and wooden shingles. It was white, trimmed with dark blue shutters. Three wooden steps led to the front door. Birdhouses of many shapes and sizes hung from the two enormous apple trees that stood in the front yard on either side of the entrance. I heard the noisy yelps of small dogs from the inside of the house.

"Those are our babies calling to us." Brain smiled widely as she listened to the dogs' increasingly loud cries. "They can sense our presence. They wonder why we aren't coming in." She laughed.

"We couldn't have kids. We wanted children desperately, but we couldn't have our own. And because of my condition, they wouldn't let us adopt. So we have dogs. Five of them. And three hairball factories, the cats. Isn't that crazy?"

I nodded weakly, uncertain if it was rude to agree with her.

"The dogs, they're all lap dogs. Little guys. All five of them try to sit in my lap at once. It's fun but a little risky. They have toppled my chair once or twice."

Brain laughed again. "It's worth it. Their kisses make everything feel better. We love the little tykes. Just as if they are our babies."

When we reached Andy's house, Crane lifted the wheelchair up the front steps and opened the door. He did not ring the doorbell or knock on the door. Obviously they had been to Andy's house before.

Brain sat in the entrance to Andy's house with the front door ajar. She said, "I want you and Crane to sit on the steps while I talk to Andy. It'll only be a few minutes."

I was afraid. Would she tell Andy she had seen my black eye and knew what had happened? I visualized Andy's rage when her cruelty was exposed. I suddenly regretted divulging my secret. I wanted to tell Brain not to say anything to Andy about what I had told her. Brain seemed to sense my panic.

"Don't worry," Brain said soothingly. She reached out to gently caress my bruised cheek. "It will be all right when you come back in the house. Trust me. I know how to talk to Andy."

Crane and I sat on the steps, as we had been instructed to do. He resumed reading his book. I strained to hear what the voices inside were saying. I could hear Brain's voice, calm but fervent. Andy was unusually quiet. I could not make out what they were saying.

After several minutes, Brain rolled out the front door to the steps.

"You can go in now," she said to me. "Andy and I have had a talk. She knows that this, this hitting, has got to stop. She blames herself, not you. She is ashamed that she hit you. She doesn't want the furies to happen ever again."

Brain hesitated. "In the morning, say nine o'clock, Crane and I will come here to take you both to my Aunt Thelma. Thelma will find out what's going on, why Andy has the furies these days. She will make it better for both of you."

Brain bent her head toward the lower step where I was sitting and kissed my cheek. Crane reached up to retrieve Brain and her chair. He placed them on the sidewalk. Brain blew me a kiss as they began walking up the street toward the little white house with the many animals.

"Good-bye new friend," Brain called as they disappeared around the corner.

I entered the house nervously. Andy was waiting. She came toward me. I flinched, waiting for her hand to strike. Instead, she said, "Brain tells me that you are lonely. I thought you might like to telephone your family."

Telephoning long-distance was a considerable expense back then in the sixties. It was reserved for momentous occasions like Christmas and

Malignant Memory

the announcement of deaths. Andy was frugal, the outcome of having to live in poverty for most of her life, I suppose. I could not believe that she would spend money in such a frivolous way.

Andy went to the telephone in the kitchen and began dialing the farm's number. I heard her say, "I won't talk now. Elizabeth would like to talk."

Mother shrieked when she heard my voice. She repeated, over and over again, how much they missed me. She told me that the snow was almost gone, that they had a new calf, that my brothers were complaining about her cooking, and that the neighbours had asked about me. She asked how I was, what I had been doing. She barely waited for my answer before she fired off another question. She asked about how it was living in Kingsford, how I found the school, if I had made friends, what I missed on the farm. She said she was proud of me for getting the marks I did. She thanked me for my letters. "I know we don't write much, but when we get your letters, we read them as a family, over and over again."

I gulped several times so that Mother would not hear tears in my voice. "I am fine," I told her. "I have a new friend. She is the librarian. I am going to go to the library with her next week. Tomorrow she's taking Andy and me to visit her aunt."

Andy stayed close by me throughout the phone call. I wondered if she was waiting to hear if I told my family about the beatings.

Mother handed the telephone to my oldest brother. Jonathan said very little. "I miss you Sis." He handed the phone to another brother. The younger boys were so eager to tell me all their news that they spoke too rapidly for me to catch what they were saying. "Slow down," I said to one of them. "It's not a race. Speak more slowly so I can understand you."

My little brothers told me about rabbits that had nested in the barn, an owl that shrieked every night, a fight between two boys at school, and the death of one of our horses. Each one ended their call by telling me they missed me.

Father was last. He told me to study hard and be good. He sounded tired, depressed.

Too soon, the call was over. I held the telephone receiver in my hand for several minutes before I hung up, letting the emotions flood me. The connection with my family had restored my soul. I was deeply loved.

Brain and Crane

I was not alone. I missed my family. But I was going to be all right.

"Thank you," I told Andy. "That was very kind of you."

She nodded. "Let's phone them once a week."

I paused and then armed with a new confidence and the knowledge that Andy was more acquiescent than usual, I blurted, "I am a good cook. I like cooking. Can I make supper tonight?"

Remarkably, Andy agreed. We went to the store to buy groceries together. Andy did not so much as grimace at my purchases. She helped me bag the apples, carrots, and potatoes. I had not seen a fresh vegetable or fruit for several months. Carrots and potatoes seemed like precious treasure to me.

I cooked a roast chicken with baked potatoes and honeyed carrots. I made rolls and apple pie. The house smelled divine.

Andy had second helpings of the meal. She raved about how good it was. She patted her stomach as she placed the leftovers in the refrigerator. "I am going to need new clothes if you keep cooking like this." I found her in the kitchen before bedtime, helping herself to another piece of pie.

Just like that, I became the cook in our house. Timidly at first and then with greater assurance, I began to think that I would someday feel at home with Andy.

CHAPTER SIX

A NEW REALITY

Once in a while, something happens to turn your world upside down. You see things with a new clarity. You wonder if you have ever truly understood the ways things are before that point. My visit to Brain's aunt was just such an occasion.

Andy was unusually quiet at breakfast. She picked at the pancakes I had made, eating little. Her coffee grew cold in the cup.

I was fearful at first, worried that her silence might be a sign of an impending assault. After some time, I realized that she was simply pensive. I was not going to be hit. I breathed a sigh of relief. I ate my pancakes eagerly.

"How do you know Brain's aunt?" I asked Andy.

"We have known each other for a long time. I met Thelma when I was first married. Your grandfather and her husband were friends. They had been friends since they were babies. Both men died in the same year."

Andy stopped. She looked into the distance without seeing.

"Thelma understands things about me that other people don't. She's experienced some of the same kind of things that I have. She doesn't judge me. She understands why I am the way I am. I trust Thelma."

Crane called to us from the front steps, precisely at nine o'clock. "Ready for a ride in the country?" he shouted cheerfully.

It was a beautiful spring day, unseasonably warm. The snow that remained on the sidewalks had turned to a grey slush in the heat of the sun. The birds serenaded us with songs of promise. I was filled with optimism. It was going to be a good day.

"Good morning, friend," Brain called to me. She was sitting in the front seat of a Valiant station wagon, white with red and white leather seats. The car was sleek, shiny, and elegant. It had a wide aluminum grill in the front that made it look like it was grinning. I had no idea a car could look so beautiful.

"Do you like it?" Crane asked shyly. "Just got it last week." I nodded, speechless.

Crane opened the side door of the car for Andy. I was about to follow her when he winked and said, "Not you. You come with me." He walked to the back of the wagon and opened the tailgate. I climbed in and sat beside Brain's wheelchair in the trunk. Crane turned a key and opened the window. "You can watch out here," he told me. "You'll get a good view of the countryside." I sat on my heels, my arms folded across the window ledge, prepared to see the world unfold before me.

We drove for several miles. Andy talked non-stop. She was our self-appointed tour guide.

"That's the Beagle House. That family has always owned beagles. And they name each one Sugar. There's Sugar 1, Sugar 2. You get the picture. They are up to Sugar 27 now. Some nights, you can hear all their beagles howling at once. People who are new to Kingsford think it's wolves howling. But it's only the Sugars."

"You can see the Indian reserve from the top of that hill. They are Cree people. They used to live right where the town is now, but the government wanted their land so they moved them here. They used to be able to farm and fish on their land. Now they live on rocky ground, mostly shale. You can't farm there. They live by the river, down from the pulp mill. The mill pumped stuff into the river. It destroyed the fish. Now the people can't fish and they can't farm.

"That tree, the big elm you see to your left, that's the tree that my husband Arthur loved above all other trees. Isn't it majestic? I am sure that tree is over a hundred years old. Imagine what it has witnessed in its lifetime!"

Brain and Crane listened attentively to Andy's travelogue, as if they had no prior knowledge of the things she told them. I was to learn later that Andy provided the same lecture every time she drove to Thelma's.

Crane stopped the car in front of a sprawling old house beside a peaceful lake. The house had seen many owners in its almost two

A New Reality

centuries of existence. Each owner had personalized the house by building an addition. The additions were mismatched and awkwardly placed. A red brick kitchen jutted out at a right angle to the wooden garage. A triangular-shaped glass and stucco sun porch sat at the back corner of the grey brick living room. A bedroom overhung the sun porch, dependent on a recessed and cracked column to keep it upright. Much of the house was in desperate need of repair and paint. Despite its aberrations, the house bore a faint air of elegance; an aging, decrepit monarch content to spend her last years remembering better times.

Crane opened the tailgate to retrieve the wheelchair. He brought the chair to the passenger door. He carried Brain out of the car and placed her gently in the chair. She reached up to touch his cheek with her open hand, smiling. "Thank you, my prince." Crane bent down to kiss her full on the lips. Andy and I looked away. We pretended not to see their embrace, embarrassed to be onlookers at something so raw and intimate.

Thelma was waiting for us on the front steps. Her deep brown eyes, the colour of varnished mahogany, sparkled as she saw us.

The contrast between the tall, thin, neatly pressed Andy and the obese, squat, unkempt Thelma was striking. Thelma was short. The top of her head reached Andy's shoulder. Layers of fat in her upper arms and stomach joggled and danced as she moved. Her salt and pepper grey hair rested in a solitary dishevelled braid on her spine, hanging down to her buttocks. She wore a food-stained, dark beige, ankle-length corduroy jumper. Her blue blouse was missing two buttons; Thelma had replaced them with large pink safety pins—the kind that were used to secure babies' diapers.

Thelma reached out her massive arms to envelop us in a hug. She held on to each of us as if she would never let go. I watched, fascinated as Andy not only tolerated Thelma's embrace but leaned into it as if she was receiving healing.

Thelma greeted us in Cree. "Mino keesikaw (It is a beautiful day!)." "My dear ones," she said in English, "you give me so much pleasure by being here." She invited us into the kitchen for lunch. "The whole gang is here," she announced brightly.

Brain explained that Thelma had nine children of her own. Her sister died, leaving eight children. Thelma adopted her sister's children.

Malignant Memory

Most of Thelma's biological and adopted children were adults now. Brain said that all 17 of Thelma's children and their families were expected to come to Thelma's every day for lunch. She grinned, "Thelma's not truly happy until her whole brood is here in her house."

People of all ages crowded the kitchen. The room was heavy with the smell of smoke from the wood stove. Coffee boiling on the wood stove provided background noise to the family's joyful chatter.

Thelma motioned to a long plywood table at the centre of the kitchen. "Sit your ass over here with us." She sat at the head of the table, her enormous buttocks and thighs bulging over her chair. She smiled broadly. Andy sat at Thelma's right. Brain, Crane, and I found a place at the other end of the table.

The conversation around the kitchen table was almost impossible to follow. Everyone talked. No one seemed to listen to anyone else. The children played their games around us on the floor.

It was clear that the children were the nucleus of the room. Every few minutes, a child would ask a question or call attention to something he or she was doing. The adults immediately paused in their conversation to attend to the child.

Thelma had made bannock that morning. She offered us some. Brain smeared honey on her piece. She took a bite, closed her eyes and said dreamily, "Oh, heaven!" I tentatively bit into the warm bannock. It was delicious. "Do you think I could have the recipe?" I asked Thelma.

Everyone around the table, including Andy, laughed uproariously. They laughed and laughed. They slapped their knees. They wiped tears from their eyes. The children stood up from the floor and joined in the laughter. I looked round the room, puzzled. What was so funny?

Thelma pushed her chair away from the table. She angled her upper body toward the table, grunting as she laid her entire weight on the plywood. The family instinctively reached out to hold the table for additional stability. Thelma rocked her body to heave her massive frame to a standing position. Everyone watched her deliberate and painful effort as she walked slowly to join me at the foot of the table.

Thelma bent down to give me a hug, enveloping me in the

A New Reality

folds of her body. "Now honey, you don't mind us. Bannock has no recipe that you write down. It's in you. Not in a book. My mother taught me how to make bannock. I will teach you."

Thelma waddled to her chair at the end of the table. She beamed at her guests. "It's time for you to go now. I have things to say to Andy and her granddaughter. I will see you tomorrow."

Thelma's family evacuated the kitchen silently and quickly. Crane and Brain told me that they would be outside until Andy and I were finished talking to Thelma.

"Now," Thelma said quietly, looking directly at Andy. "I hear you have been having the furies again. It's been a long time since you've had the furies." Andy looked down at her lap.

"There's always something that makes the furies come back. Do you know what it is this time?"

Andy said nothing. She licked her lips nervously, her tongue jutting in and out of her partially closed lips in a frantic dance. She twisted the bracelet on her left wrist.

Thelma motioned to Andy. They left me to go to another room. They were gone for a long time. When they returned, Andy's eyes were red, as if she'd been crying.

Thelma held out her wide arms. "Little one, you come here." I sat awkwardly in her lap. I was much taller than her, but she held me as if I were an infant.

Thelma turned to face Andy.

"I am going to talk to the little one for a while, Andy. She needs to know why you and I are cursed with the furies."

Andy nodded. Her eyes remained downcast.

Thelma held me tight, stroking my forehead and cheeks with her fingers. The fire in the wood stove crackled and hissed.

"Little one, your grandmother and I have shared some things that should never happen to little girls. It was different for each of us, but our pain is the same. That pain causes us to do things that we are not proud of. It causes us to become angry. To have the furies so bad that nobody can reach us. When we have the furies, all we want to do is to hurt people in the way that we were hurt. We don't want to be that way, but the furies overcome us."

Thelma was quiet for several minutes. She rocked me, humming under her breath.

Malignant Memory

"Andy does not want to talk to you yet about what happened to her. She finds it too hard. But we have known each other for many years. I know parts of her story because I have told her parts of my story. I am going to tell you what I know because Andy wants me to."

I shut my eyes against Thelma's breast and waited.

"Your great-grandmother, Andy's mother, died when Andy was eight years old. They think she died of a broken heart. Andy's father, your great-grandfather, he had deserted the family the year before. No one knew where he went. Why he went. He was never heard from again. He took the baby, the only boy, Andy's brother.

"Both parents were gone. They needed to find a home for Andy and her sister, Helen. The oldest sister, Maude, was married by then, living in Ottawa. Daisy was also married. Maude had a child, Daisy was expecting. They couldn't take care of Andy. Helen was adopted by her aunt. She lived in Michigan. No one in the family wanted Andy."

Thelma paused to allow the impact of her words to settle in me. She continued, "Maude took Andy to a home for orphans in New York. The staff at the Home said they would find Andy a good home.

"The next night, a man told Andy that she was going to be adopted by someone she had not met. They gave her a bath. She got a new dress. In the morning, Andy went with many other children to the train station. They were all orphans or children whose parents couldn't look after them. There were a lot of orphans in the country, back then. Some of the children were little, three or four years old. Andy was one of the oldest. She was eight.

"The children boarded a train. There was only a couple of adults with them, staff from the Home. Most of the children had never been on a train before. Most of them had never been away from their families before. Can you imagine how frightened those little ones must have been?"

I nodded, eager to hear the rest of the story.

"The train would stop in a town. The children would get out. They would stand on a stage by the train. There were crowds of people waiting to see the children. They were there because they had seen posters saying that homes were needed for orphans. The posters announced the date and time of the train's arrival. People who wanted to adopt one of the orphans could take them right away.

A New Reality

"The people who had come to see the orphans would crowd around them, opening their mouths to check the condition of their teeth, feeling their arm muscles. Andy told me that it was horrifying having all these strangers pawing her. She hated it.

"Then someone from the town, usually the mayor, would tell the people a little about each child. The child would dance or sing to show off her or his talent. The town's official would say that the child was very strong, or very smart, or anything else to entice people to adopt her or him.

"Andy had memorized a poem, but when it came time for her to perform, she couldn't talk. She just cried. Some people in the crowd booed her.

"Andy figures the train stopped at more than thirty towns. Most of the children in her train were adopted. One boy who had crossed eyes and had seizures wasn't. Neither was Andy. When the train returned to New York, the staff at the Home declared Andy as 'unadoptable.' They notified Maude that Andy was deficient. They advised that Andy be placed in a Home for children who were slow-minded."

I gasped, outraged. I felt defensive for my grandmother. "She was just a little girl. She was scared, not stupid."

Thelma smiled gently. She patted my hand. "Maude and Daisy knew that Andy was not stupid. They decided that Andy would go to an orphanage in Ottawa, close to Maude. Andy lived there until she met your grandfather and married him." She looked toward Andy. "How old were you then, Andy? When you married Arthur?"

"Seventeen." Andy spoke so softly I had to strain to hear her.

"On her first day at the orphanage, the matron shaved Andy's hair in case she had lice. She took away the clothes she had brought from home. She had to wear a uniform, the same clothing as everyone else in the place."

Andy surprised us by interrupting. She spoke quietly but with fury in her voice. "Matron took my china doll, the one I called 'Betsy.' My father had given me that doll before he left. Maude had kept it for me. She gave it to me when I went into the orphanage. I begged Matron to give Betsy back to me. She wouldn't. I never saw that Betsy doll again."

Andy bowed her head. She spoke in a whisper. "Matron kept saying over and over that orphans were bad blood. Once, the doctor took blood from my arm. I was sure my blood would be black or green. I thought maybe my blood would have pus in it. But it was red, just like everyone else's."

Thelma waited until she was sure that Andy had nothing further to say before she continued. "It was lonely for her in that orphanage. She saw her sister Maude about once a year. Maude told Andy that she couldn't help her, that she had a family of her own to look after, that Andy should just get used to the orphanage. So here she was, just a tiny tyke, no family, her parents both gone, living with strangers."

Thelma paused. "The staff at the orphanage—some of them were kind, but some of them were very cruel. The cruel ones loved to punish the girls by shaving their hair or not giving them food. They carried leather belts wherever they went so they could strap the girls. Some made sure they hit the girls with the belt buckle so it would really hurt."

I heard Andy crying softly beside us. She stared at her lap, not looking at us.

"There was one staff member who was really cruel. It was Matron. Andy loved school, but Matron didn't think school would do Andy any good. Matron thought she was stupid. Matron made her work in the orphanage instead of going to school. Andy was expected to clean, do laundry, to do the work of an adult. They worked her to the bone."

Andy spoke again in a whisper. We strained to hear her. "Matron was really big, like a giant to us children. And so ugly. She had a mole on her cheek with a big black hair protruding from it. When she got angry, she would snort like a horse. Her face would turn a dark red, and her pupils would be like saucers. Her nostrils would get wide; the veins in her temples would throb. She would scream at us until I thought my eardrums would burst."

Andy was quiet for a few minutes. "Sometimes Matron pulled me out of bed at night. She would strap me until I bled. She wouldn't tell me what I had done. She hated me and I never knew why."

Thelma reached her hand out to stroke Andy's arm for a few minutes.

"Andy suffered much cruelty, but what was even worse was watching what some of the staff did to other girls. Sometimes it is harder to be a witness to cruelty than to experience it yourself."

Andy looked up. She spoke, tentatively at first and then

A New Reality

sharply, with bitterness. I stared at her, amazed that she was being so communicative about herself.

"There was a night watchman. He was ugly. He had pimples all over his face. He had bad breath. He would come into the dorm at night. He'd take one of the girls to his room. I'd watch him walk slowly down the line of beds, staring at each one of us until he made his choice. I'd pray that he wouldn't take me. He never did. He preferred the pretty girls.

"Whoever he chose that night would beg him to leave her alone, to take someone else. He just laughed. He dragged the girl out of her bed and down the hall. The girl wouldn't come back to the dorm until much later. Most of the time, she would be crying. Sometimes she would stare as if she weren't seeing anything. Sometimes there would be blood on her nightshirt, down her legs. She would curl up on her bed and mew like a tiny kitten. I felt so helpless, so guilty.

"Nobody told on him. He threatened to kill the girls if they squealed. I tried to tell Matron once. She said I was lying, trying to make trouble. She put me in the closet, one that was pitch dark. Matron locked it from outside. She told me there was a rat living in the closet. She knew I was petrified of rats. I had no food, no water, for two days. There was no bathroom.

"I found out later that Matron and the night watchman were cousins."

She paused. Her hands twisted nervously in her lap.

Thelma asked softly, "Do you want to tell us anything else Andy?" Andy nodded, gulping twice before she began. She spoke slowly, as if each word caused her physical pain. She paused often to breathe in sharply.

"There were seven little girls in the nursery section. It was my job to care for them. The little girls would climb on my lap and I would read them stories, brush their hair, sing them songs. I liked being with them. We were like a family.

"One little girl, she was five. Her name was Angela. We called her Angel. She was such a sweet little girl. She had gorgeous dark eyes and a smile as bright as sunshine. She smiled all the time. I loved her." Andy started to sob loudly, mucus dribbling from her nose in a steady stream. I sat still, expressionless, afraid that any motion or gesture would distract her from revealing her story. I wanted desperately to wipe the snot from her lips and chin, to help

Malignant Memory

Andy regain her usual comportment.

After some time, Andy recovered her composure with visible effort. "I was in charge of the little girls' baths. They had a bath once a month. A big tub was brought into the kitchen. I was supposed to fill it with water from a big kettle. This particular Saturday, the kettle was on the stove, heating. The tub was in the middle of the kitchen, waiting to be filled. I helped the little girls take off their clothes.

"We were all very hungry, the little girls and me. They hardly fed us in the orphanage. We never had enough food. And the food they gave us was awful. Once, our porridge had maggots floating in it!

"We were always hungry, always thinking about food.

"Angel asked me if I had any food in my pockets. I didn't. Sometimes I used to steal food from the plates after a meal was over, and I'd share it with them. I had no food in my pockets this night.

"I imagined what would be behind the cupboard doors. I saw jams and cookies and pickles, and all good things to eat in my imagination. I couldn't stop thinking about the food in the cupboards.

"I was willing to risk everything just for a bite of food.

"I tried the cupboards just to see. One door opened. They usually locked all the cupboards but this time, they had forgotten one cupboard.

"I knew I'd get in trouble, but I didn't care. I found a tin of crackers. It was full. I held out the open tin to the little girls. I told them to eat as much as they wanted. The little girls squealed with delight. They were so excited."

Andy was quiet for so long that I began to think that she had decided not to continue. She stared into the room, not seeing. Haltingly, she began again.

"We were like wolves, devouring those crackers. There were crumbs everywhere, on the floor, on the shelves, on our clothes. We gobbled up everything in that tin as fast as we could. Nothing had ever tasted as good as those dry old crackers.

"Then I heard Matron's footsteps.

"Matron was a big woman. Her footsteps were heavy. I could hear her plod, plod down the hallway. She was coming closer and closer to the kitchen.

"The little girls heard Matron approaching. They began to whimper. They knew how mean she could be.

"I yelled at the little girls to get rid of the crumbs. They scurried to

A New Reality

brush the crumbs away, to hide them in their pockets and shoes. I hid the empty cracker tin beneath the pile of bath towels. We were scampering around the kitchen, almost falling on top of each other, madly trying to hide the evidence of our crime.

"I told Angel to take off her nightdress and get into the tub. She sat in the tub, waiting. She was smiling.

"I ran to the stove to get the water to fill the tub. I was panicking now. I knew if we got caught, we'd be beaten. I had learned how to make my mind travel away from the beating when it happened to me. I had not learned how to distance myself from watching it happen to others, especially the younger girls. I couldn't bear to watch Matron beat the little girls with her strap.

"I grabbed the kettle. I quickly poured the water in the tub. I poured it over Angel. Angel started screaming. It was a scream of pure agony. The water was boiling hot."

Andy put her face in her hands. She wept loudly, her words muffled in her heaving sobs. "Angel threw herself against both sides of the tub, as if she were having a fit. She screamed and screamed. She screamed like a wounded cat. I still hear that scream sometimes in my sleep.

"I couldn't move. I stood stupidly by the tub. I was paralyzed.

"The little girls started to shriek. They begged me to help Angel. One put a towel in my hands. She motioned for me to take Angel out of the boiling water. It startled me out of my trance. I reached out to hold Angel, to get her out of the tub. Her skin fell off in the towel.

"I looked at the towel, not comprehending what I was seeing. My brain slowly allowed the realization of what had happened to enter my consciousness. I was filled with horror. One of the little girls fainted.

"Angel had stopped screaming. She was eerily quiet. She wasn't moving. Just then, Matron opened the door. She looked furious."

Andy cried noisily, tears and snot running from her face to the front of her dress. I went to console her. Thelma held me tighter. "Let her be, little one. She needs to get this story told."

After what seemed like an eternity, Andy began again. "Matron told me to go to her office. I kept replaying Angel's screams in my mind. I wanted to die. I had burned that sweet little girl. I thought any punishment was too good for me. I prayed that Matron would make me suffer as much as Angel had suffered.

Malignant Memory

"Matron would not answer my questions about Angel. Whether she was alive. If she'd be okay. Matron hit me with the strap on my face, over my head, on my arms and chest. I am sure she beat me for over an hour. Finally, I lost consciousness. When I came to, my ears were bleeding. I never heard properly after that."

I caught my breath. I suddenly understood why Andy talked all the time. If you are talking, you don't have to listen, to admit you can't hear.

Andy's voice was tremulous. "Angel was in the infirmary. They wouldn't let me see her. I was not allowed to look after the little girls anymore. The girl who was assigned to the nursery after me told me the little girls started sucking their thumbs, wetting their beds, having nightmares about me burning Angel. They did not play. They were too quiet. When the little girls saw me in the orphanage, they looked scared. They did not speak to me.

"Matron called me into her office a week later. She told me that Angel had died. She said I had killed her. She said I was evil. As punishment, she made me stand on one foot without any clothes every night after the others had gone to bed. Matron sat in a chair while I stood on the cold hallway floor, shivering. She taunted me, called me names. Said I was going to hell. She beat me whenever I let my other foot touch the floor. She only let me sleep when she got too tired to stay awake. It went on for weeks."

Andy said hoarsely, as if in disbelief, "I was only nine years old." The unspeakable horror of Andy's story left me transfixed and speechless, unable to do anything but watch helplessly as Andy's shoulders heaved.

Thelma shifted my weight to stand me beside her chair. Thelma turned to her friend. "Come here, Andy. Come to Thelma," she crooned as she cradled Andy's head and shoulders. Gradually, Andy's tears became more muffled, less desperate. Thelma turned to me.

"Andy has more stories like this one. She tries to bury these stories but they wait in her, ready to destroy her when she isn't ready. Then they come out with a vengeance. She gets the furies. People like Andy and I, we are damaged people. Because of what we experienced, we walk around with a lump of ice in our hearts. The ice never melts. It affects everything we do, everything we are.

"I am going to talk to Andy now, little one. I want to find out

A New Reality

why the furies have returned. You go outside with Brain and Crane. I will call you when we are ready."

I realized only then that my cheeks were drenched with tears. Nothing in my sheltered life had prepared me for Andy's story. How, I wondered, was it possible for Andy to live life in an ordinary way after something of such magnitude occurred to her? Surely she would never be the same again.

I walked to the front door, my heart heavy with grief for my grandmother, for Angel, for all those who were victims of senseless aggression.

Brain and Crane walked me to the lake to look at the birds nesting by the shore. They asked no questions. Brain prattled about the birds, listing the species she saw. I could barely attend to what she was saying. I replayed the stories Andy had told me over and over again in my mind. I was so intent in my recollections, that for a minute I forgot that Brain and Crane were not with me in my head.

I blurted, "How could the people at the orphanage have treated a child like Andy so cruelly? Why didn't the other staff report the staff who were so cruel to the orphans?"

Brain looked at me sadly. "It is so hard to understand, isn't it? I remember listening to Thelma and Andy when I was young and just being horrified that anyone could do those things to children. I don't think I will ever understand why it happened. Why no one in the orphanage or in the residential school stopped it."

I told Brain that I could not comprehend such heartlessness. I told her that I could never treat another person so cruelly.

Crane turned from looking at the lake to face me directly. He spoke softly but firmly.

"All of us have the capacity to be cruel. We may not beat anyone or hurt them physically, but we are all capable of making others suffer. Every time we regard someone else as different, as less than us, we are capable of treating them in ways that are unkind. A mean word, a dismissive glance. Not including somebody. Treating them as if they are stupid. These are cruelties that we can inflict on others when we see their difference as unacceptable."

My cheeks reddened. I wanted to disagree with him, to assure him that cruelty was beyond me. But the image of Hannah Austin

Malignant Memory

entered my consciousness.

I turned once more to stare in silence at the lake. After more than an hour, Thelma called to us to come inside. Andy's eyes were red-rimmed. She looked exhausted.

"I have something to tell you," Thelma announced when we were seated in the kitchen. "Andy has had the furies lately because she has been upset. Very upset, distraught." She turned to face me directly. "Do you remember me telling you that Andy's father left and she never saw him again? Well, he's been found. He's in a hospital in New York. He has no money, no home. He's an old man. He had a stroke. He can't talk. He needs someone to look after him. He has no one to care for him except Andy."

Brain and I gasped. Crane stood silently in the doorway. Thelma added, angrily, "You can understand why Andy is upset. It is her father's fault that she went to the orphanage after her mother died. She hates him for what he did to her mother, to her. He did nothing for her all these years. He has not been part of her life. He knows nothing about her. She doesn't know him. Now she is expected to look after him."

"Can't Andy's sisters look after him?" I asked timidly.

"Maude's husband is ill. She can't manage another person to look after. Helen died. Then there's Daisy. She lives in Toronto. But Daisy's husband won't have their father live with them. He has refused. He's a mean bugger, that husband. Anyway, Andy's father's arriving from New York at the end of July."

I had so many questions. One look at Thelma's face told me not to ask them; this wasn't the time. I couldn't restrain myself. I looked toward Andy. "Our house is small. Where would he sleep? I am in school all day. You are busy with the church and the neighbours. Who will look after him?"

Andy looked startled, as if she had not thought about such practicalities. Thelma stared at me as if to warn me that I should not ask any more questions. I was silent.

Brain said, "We'll help. Crane and I will help you and Andy figure this out. We have four months to get ready."

Thelma hugged me. She smiled, "Don't worry. We'll all help." She addressed Brain and Crane, "These two have had a heavy day. They need to go home to rest. I will put some soup and bannock in a bag for their

A New Reality

dinner. They need to let what we talked about settle in for a while. Then maybe you could bring them back here tomorrow?"

Brain nodded.

The trip back to Andy's house was quiet. No one spoke. I sat in the back seat of the new car beside Andy. She looked out the side window, not seeing. I reached over and held her hand. We held hands without speaking all the way home.

CHAPTER SEVEN

MAGNANIMITY

It is a profoundly beautiful thing to witness kindness given without expectation of reciprocity or the need for acknowledgement. Andy and I were the grateful recipients of such benevolence in the coming months. We became stronger, happier, and more peaceful in ourselves and with each other because of the unconditional kindnesses that Brain, Crane, and Thelma gave to us.

Crane drove Andy to visit Thelma every afternoon. Andy would return home too exhausted to speak. She never revealed what had occurred in these visits. Gradually, she began to sleep better, to be less restless. She ate with gusto the meals I prepared. Soon her formerly hallowed face was fuller, softer. Her cheeks were no longer unnaturally pale. Her skin had a soft pink hue.

Andy initiated a practice of hugging me every night before I went to bed. Initially, her hugs were awkward and forced. They seemed more like assigned homework than genuine signs of affection. I imagined that Andy was enacting Thelma's suggestions for remediation.

After several weeks, Andy's bedtime hugs became more natural, less contrived. They eventually became comforting, something I looked forward to. Occasionally Andy hugged me spontaneously at other times of the day. Once I was ill with a cold. Andy stroked my forehead with her palm. She kissed my eyelids when she thought I was sleeping.

Slowly and reticently over the next months Andy began to volunteer some of the stories about her past. Many of them were about the hardships she had experienced as an orphan and then later as a widow. The stories helped me to understand her in a new way.

Malignant Memory

They helped me to make sense of some of her peculiarities, like her habit of checking the contents of closets every night and refusing to close the bathroom door. Understanding birthed a compassion and care for Andy that I had not previously experienced.

One of Andy's stories was about how she met my grandfather.

"The orphanage would have these events, visiting days, like open houses, where rich people could come and see why they should give money to the orphanage. Matron would make sure we were clean and nicely dressed. She would tell us that we should say that we were grateful for the loving care we received from the staff, especially her. We knew we would be beaten if we didn't do as she said.

"Your grandfather came one visiting day. He was much older than I was. Twenty years older. I thought he was a rich dignitary. The visitors paraded in front of the line of orphans, asking questions. 'How old are you?' 'How long have you been at the orphanage?' 'What do you like best about the orphanage?'

"Then your grandfather was standing in front of me. He took my hands in his. He had the gentlest eyes. He was elegant, handsome.

"He said, 'I had to meet you. I think you are one of the loveliest young women I have ever seen.' I blushed. I was so embarrassed. I thought maybe he had problems with his vision. But then I was excited. I was going to be eighteen in a few months, the time I would have to leave the orphanage. I knew that I wouldn't be able to get any kind of decent job outside the orphanage without an education or any training. Marriage seemed the only viable option, but I wasn't sure anyone would want me.

"Turned out that Arthur wasn't rich. He'd come with his uncle. His uncle was rich, not Arthur.

"I married Arthur six weeks later. I didn't love him then, but I grew to love him. I never regretted marrying him. He was the first person in a long time who saw beauty in me. He loved me completely, even with all my faults. Even with the furies.

"Right before we were to be married, Arthur bought me a china doll, Betsy, the doll you have now. He told me that he was sorry he couldn't give me the doll my father had given me, the one they took away at the orphanage. He wanted me to have a reminder that new beginnings were possible. He wanted me to know I was loved."

Magnanimity

Some of my favourite times during those months waiting for Great-Grandfather were when I visited with Brain and Crane in their home that was crowded with books and pets. Brain and Crane always acted delighted to see me. The little dogs yammered for attention. The cats ignored us.

It was Brain who I really came to see. I was fascinated by Brain's determination to live her life as if her twisted limbs presented no encumbrances. I had never known a person in a wheelchair before. Crane helped Brain to navigate stairs, but Brain was fiercely independent in most other ways. She was fond of saying, "If I can possibly do it myself, I will." Her arms were incredibly strong. She could propel herself up to her bed or the kitchen counter from her chair without anyone's assistance, and with seeming ease.

My greatest attraction to Brain was her affirmation of myself. I had never experienced an adult who was so interested in who I was, so fascinated with what was happening in my life. Brain was my confidante, someone who affirmed who I was, who thought I was special, gifted. Her esteem and appreciation of me was seductive.

Crane was pleasant to me, but he was often preoccupied, cooking the meals, cleaning the house, doing yard work, or reading. Brain and I would plead with him to join us, but Crane simply smiled and carried on what he was doing.

Brain and Crane's house was filled with love; love for their pets, their visitors, but mostly for each other. Andy said once, "I love that Brain and Crane are so in love. They don't seem to mind showing the whole world that they care deeply about one another." Even small, seemingly tedious tasks that they shared together were opportunities for Brain and Crane to express their love for one another. Crane would stroke Brain's cheek with his index finger. Brain would rest her head on his lap. They called each other "My love," "Dearest one," "Love of my life."

One of Brain's and my favourite pastimes was to play chess. Brain had played it since she was a child. Her mathematical prowess was a perfect fit for chess. She became adept at the game by the time she was an adolescent. No one in Kingsford could beat her record of wins.

"Chess is an allegory of life," Brain often said. "Just like in life, you have opponents and you have protectors. You need to know who's who. And you need to be willing to wait to make decisions, not to just

Malignant Memory

jump in and do something. In chess, you need to take in the whole board, not just the pieces. In life, you need to see the whole picture, not just what's directly in front of you. And in life, you have to be ready to lose in the short term in order to win in the long term."

Brain was a patient but unrelenting teacher. She demanded excellence. She commanded me to be a tactical and strategic player. She did not let me win just because I was younger and less experienced. We both understood that I would have to deserve a win.

My first games of chess with Brain were agonizing. It seemed as if I would never learn how the Bishop was different from a Knight. I played without a plan, reacting to Brain's moves without strategizing my defence. I often moved my Queen out too quickly, a sure sign of a beginner player. In those first games, Brain would declare, "Checkmate!" after I had only made a few moves.

We debriefed after every game. Although it was humiliating to lose, Brain would point out how I was making gradual improvements. I was thrilled when I won my first game. Crane made us lemonade to celebrate the victory. I did not win another game for several weeks.

Andy and I spent a great deal of time with Brain and Crane that summer. We saw them almost every day. They held a surprise birthday party for us at their house. Crane drove Thelma into Kingsford to join us. We had cake with candles and homemade ice cream. Brain and Crane gave me two volumes of Shakespeare's plays as a present. Andy presented me with a store-bought dress that fit. Thelma gave me some strawberry jam she had preserved.

After dinner, we danced to music Crane played on a record player. Crane held the arms of Brain's wheelchair as they danced around the living room. Andy, Thelma and I smiled at the joy and love on their faces as they danced. My wish as I blew out the candles on the cake was to experience a love like theirs one day.

There were many decisions to be made in preparation for Great-Grandfather's stay as July loomed. Andy referred to him not by his name or as her father. "The Poor Excuse for a Man," "The Worm," and "Satan" were her favourite descriptors. She contorted her face in rage whenever she spoke of him.

Conversations between Andy and me often turned to what we would need to accommodate Great-Grandfather in our home.

Magnanimity

Sometimes what Great-Grandfather would need seemed overwhelming. Andy and I barely knew where to begin.

Andy acknowledged that she would have to stay home more to care for Great-Grandfather. "The neighbours will just have to do without me for a while. I need to look after the Worm. I have to do it. It's my duty. The bible says to honour your mother and father. I will look after him because I try to be a good Christian. Not because I love him." She added spitefully, "But I don't have to like that he's here."

Somewhat reluctantly, Andy recognized that she would need to hear better to care for her father. "Thelma says that he's eighty-seven years old and he might fall in the night. I wouldn't hear him. He might bleed to death because of a fall. I wouldn't care, but my sisters would blame me. They still love him, even after what he did to my mother, to us. They would give me no end of grief if something were to happen to Satan."

Crane took Andy to a hearing specialist. The specialist said she was profoundly deaf in her right ear, slightly deaf in her left ear. The specialist prescribed a hearing aid. He said that the newest hearing aids were an improvement on their predecessors. They could be worn discreetly behind the wearer's ear.

Andy hated the hearing aid at first. It was larger and more visible than she had expected. "Everyone will know I am deaf when they see that thing sticking out behind my ear." She loathed how the hearing aid exaggerated every sound, including background noises. "I didn't want to hear everything. I didn't want to hear the traffic outside, the furnace, the dogs barking. I just wanted to know what people are saying."

Andy adjusted to the hearing aid in a few short weeks. I overheard her telling a neighbour that the hearing aid was a blessing. "I don't know why people hesitate to get one if they need it. I can hear what people are saying to me. I missed a lot of things before." She reminded people to speak to her left side, "the better side."

Sleeping arrangements after Great-Grandfather's arrival were an issue for Andy. She was vehement that her father could not sleep in the same room as me. She categorically refused to give up her bedroom for "the horrible old geezer." Crane arrived at a solution that met Andy's approval. He built an addition at the back of the house that held two bedrooms, one for me and one for Great-Grandfather. He argued that my current bedroom was too small to contain the mountains of books

Malignant Memory

I was bringing home from the library. He pointed out that I would need space to entertain my new friends in our home.

Crane and his many friends laboured to build the addition. They installed large windows on three sides of the addition, providing much-needed natural light in the house. Each room contained a large closet. For the first time, I could hang my clothes instead of folding them in the roll-top desk drawers. Great-Grandfather's bedroom was separated from mine by a small corridor.

Crane built bookcases for me that covered an entire wall of my new bedroom. "To hold your many books," he teased. He moved the roll-top desk from the old bedroom to the new one when I said that I loved having the desk nearby. "It reminds me of my grandfather," I told him.

Crane lifted Brain up the front steps of Andy's house when the addition was complete. She applauded when she saw the craftsmanship. "It's beautiful, Crane. Absolutely beautiful! You are a treasure." They kissed. Brain stroked his face with her palm. "You are so wonderful," she told him lovingly. "What would I ever do without you?"

I met Brain and Crane at the library almost every day. I loved that library. It was my special place, my sanctuary, my safe haven. The century-old, red brick library building was magnificent. Everything about the library, from the thick, twisted vines that formed an archway over the front entrance to the stained glass windows depicting celebrated literary figures, promised an extraordinary experience to those who entered.

Inside the library was a splendid, heavy cast iron staircase that wound upward to the second and third floors. Murals depicting the disciplines of literature, philosophy, and science adorned the walls along the staircase. A turnstile at the entrance to the stacks counted the number of book borrowers. Heavy wooden bookcases extended from floor to ceiling, separated by narrow corridors. Obese patrons were required to move sideways when searching for a book.

I have experienced few pleasures in life as deep and sustaining as being in that elegant library, unconstrained by time limits or by assigned reading. I spent most of my time crouched on the floor of the musty stacks or walking between the bookcases. I riffled through books, fingering their spines, opening them at random to read a page or two, and then replacing them tenderly on the shelf.

I read voraciously. I read books that were deep and ponderous,

Magnanimity

books that helped me to see life in new ways, and books that were silly and superficial. I read children's books and books meant for someone much older than I. In the pages of those books, I grew up. I explored who I was and who I wanted to become. I discovered what I believed and what beliefs I could not support. I birthed new questions and sought the answers.

Brain introduced me to the Dewey Decimal system of cataloguing books. Initially, she would give me a new Dewey Decimal challenge every day. "Find a book on humpback whales." "Where would you locate a book on Egyptian mummies?" I giggled when I discovered that religion could be found in the BS section of the library.

Brain's desk was opposite the front entrance, on the main floor. There was always a long line in front of the desk of people wanting to talk to Brain. The line snaked around the first floor of the library, crowding the access to the stacks. Brain knew the name of every one of the people who lined up. She remembered details about their lives, often inquiring about their family and pets.

Brain had a rare gift. She could make every person she talked to feel like they were special. She responded with rapt attention to anyone who talked to her, even if what they said was trivial or superficial. She acted as though she was privileged by their presence. I marvelled at her ability to treat each customer as the most important person in her day. Young and old alike relished their time with her.

Crane sat at a table in front of Brain's desk at the library, reading and waiting for Brain to indicate that she needed him to fetch something or lift her up the stairs. Crane and I rarely spoke, but sometimes he would hand me a book and say, "Thought you might like to read this." He was never wrong in his choice of books for me. I loved them all.

Crane had an endearing habit of writing little notes and placing them in books for a reader to discover. Brain told me about Crane's practice of leaving secret notes, but it took many weeks before I found one. It was in Morton Thompson's Not as a Stranger. The note read, "Do you ever wonder why the protagonist in the story, Lucas Marsh, took so long to realize that he, like all of us, needs the care and compassion of other people? He was not a stupid man. He was a skilled physician. But he was stupid about this essential fact of life. I wonder, too, if he would have ever recognized that no man is an island without the dogged devotion of his wife to dissuade him from his delusions of independence. I wonder about these things every time I read this wonderful book. Signed, a friend."

Thanks to Crane, I was introduced to many subjects I might otherwise have overlooked, such as science fiction and archeology. He was the one who introduced me to the poetry of Elizabeth Barrett Browning. Crane called her EBB. I loved the story of the romance of Elizabeth Barrett and Robert Browning. I thought it fortuitous that EBB's sister had the same name as my grandmother, Henrietta.

I began to quote EBB at every available occasion. When Brain suggested I was procrastinating writing a letter to my family by looking up random words in the dictionary, I told her, "At painful times, when composition is impossible and reading is not enough, grammars and dictionaries are excellent for distraction." When Andy announced that we would have an unexpected visit from Thelma, I said, "God answers sharp and sudden on some prayers, And thrusts the thing we have prayed for in our face, A gauntlet with a gift in it." When Crane commented that my take on the Shakespearian play Hamlet was "unusual," I responded curtly, "What is genius but the power of expressing a new individuality?"

I was obnoxious in my newfound obsession.

Andy, Brain, and Crane were patient with me, waiting for my crush on EBB to fade. But despite Brain and Crane's efforts to introduce me to other female authors and Crane's suggestion that EBB's poetry was "overly romantic," my fervour did not lessen.

Brain decided to call me by the nickname EBB's family had given her. Soon all those who knew me in Kingsford, including Andy, called me Ba.

I took home a bag heavy with books every day after my time in the library. Brain would stamp the card at the back of each book with the date. I would sign the card. I loved reading the names on the cards of the people who had taken out the book before me. Sometimes I recognized a neighbour's name or that of a classmate or a teacher. Taking out an old book that had an empty card felt as though I was giving that book life. Once I took out a book by Martin Buber that had not been signed out for 30 years. I looked at the signature. It was my grandfather's name, Arthur Anderson. I was thrilled to have this tenuous connection with him, to know that we shared similar tastes in books.

Magnanimity

I learned that some truly great books were rarely taken out of the library. Moby Dick, for example, was ignored by library patrons for months at a time. It became clear that although many people cited this amazing book and some knew its storyline, few actually read it.

Hannah Austin was a regular visitor to the library and like me, an avid reader. It was Brain who helped me appreciate Hannah in a new way. Brain called me over to her desk one day, saying, "Come over here. I have someone I want you to meet." She introduced me to Hannah, as if we had never met. She told Hannah that I was bright and creative. She bragged of my abilities as a scholar and my integrity as a person. She told me, "Hannah's a very intelligent girl, a 'bookhead,' just like you. You and she have a lot in common. Tell Hannah what you discovered last week about shrunken heads."

I soon discovered that Hannah was a different person in the context of Brain's admiration and delight. She was less cynical, less bent on shocking people, more willing to engage in dialogue. With Brain as our choreographer, Hannah and I came to recognize our similarities. We became friends. I was no longer afraid of her.

Like me, Hannah appreciated a world in which books were more important than movie stars or pop music. We were the outcasts, the ones who didn't fit in among our peers. Occasionally we admitted to one another that we secretly suspected we were not worthy enough to be included with our more popular classmates. Together we were able to experience belonging.

Brain and Crane took me to pick paint for my new bedroom in Andy's house when the room was completed. I chose mint green. Brain sewed curtains and a bedspread with green and pink flowers to match the newly painted walls. "We'll have to get you a new bed to fit the bedspread I made," Brain said. She winked at me.

Brain's parents had moved to Arizona the previous year for her mother's health. They had stored their furniture in a large shed behind Brain and Crane's house, thinking that they might return to Kingsford eventually. Brain's mother had died in Arizona. Her father had decided to live there permanently.

Brain told Andy, "My father wants me to give their furniture away. I think, Andy, that you and Ba could use some of it. Ba needs a new bed and I think that an elderly man like your father should have a real bed, not an army cot." I nodded, agreeing. Even my slight frame caused the cot to bow almost to the floor.

Andy surprised me by responding cheerfully, "That would be lovely, Brain. Ba can help you pick out things that might look good in our house."

The shed was packed to the rafters full of treasures. It held a trove of handsome furniture, much of it more than a century old. I squealed with delight as I began pointing to items I particularly liked. Crane moved the objects to the yard so that we could examine them more fully. Soon the backyard was scattered with furniture.

We located a canopy maple bed with spiral-decorated pillars for my new bedroom. The circular arched headboard and footboard were decorated in an elaborate design of mother of pearl inlay. A matching tall-boy dresser and a bedside table completed the set. Crane found a bed that Great-Grandfather could use. "It's perfect," he declared. "It has a great mattress that will give his back good support." We found lamps, a dresser for Great-Grandfather's bedroom, and paintings by unknown artists.

"My mother loved art," Brain told me. "She had good taste, don't you think? That picture over there," she pointed to a framed landscape lying at the corner of the backyard, "would look really nice in your new bedroom. My mother would have liked knowing that you had one of her favourite paintings."

Andy visited the shed for herself when she discovered how amazing our finds were. She took away a Duncan Phyfe mahogany dropleaf table and six chairs with cane backing. "It's time to retire our little kitchen table," she announced to Brain. "Now we can have visitors. Ba's cooking deserves to be shared with others who will enjoy it as much as I have." Andy gently squeezed my shoulder in an affectionate gesture.

Andy located a blue and white couch, burgundy wingback chairs, and cream-coloured lamps in the shed. "I think my living room needs a new beginning," she said. She also claimed nesting tables, a beautiful maple coffee table with gold claw feet, and an old steamer trunk embossed in tin with butterflies. She said no to a new bedroom set. "Your grandfather and I slept in that bed on our wedding night and for all the years after that. It's the only bed I want."

Crane pointed to a large Persian rug with shades of purple,

Magnanimity

burgundy and blue. "I think this might be nice in your living room," he said to Andy. She nodded, her eyes watered.

Andy's house was revitalized by all the changes. It no longer looked crowded and dingy, but bright and airy. The dull living room was painted a light grey. A painting of Texas bluebells hung over the new couch.

Brain managed to convince Andy to put only some of her many photographs on the walls. "People will notice them more if there are only a few," she said persuasively. She found frames for the photos Andy chose. The other photographs were stored in albums. Jesus was relegated to the attic.

Great-Grandfather's bedroom looked warm and inviting when it was finished. Crane had painted it sunshine yellow. Brain sewed a new bedspread and curtains for the room in a dark blue and pale yellow plaid. "We'll ask him when he comes what pictures he would like on the walls." Andy responded with a loud, "Hmph! As if the Worm has any choice in what I give him. He's lucky I am letting him stay with us."

I moved into my new bedroom in early July. I had never slept in such a palatial room. I lay in that bed early in the morning and I felt I was truly a queen. I half expected servants to greet me, bring me my breakfast, and lay out my clothes for the day. I danced in my nightgown in front of the windows, embracing the sunlight. Crane had hung a bird feeder by one of the windows. I watched a tiny hummingbird zinging her way to and from the feeder. I felt profoundly spoiled and very happy.

Being at home with Andy was increasingly comfortable. We enjoyed each other's company more and more. Sometimes Andy chose to spend time with me rather than minister to a neighbour. She even missed Mass occasionally. "I am learning that God doesn't expect me to make amends all my life." She never said why she should make amends or how she had arrived at this insight.

The weekly telephone calls to my family were no longer followed by deep loneliness and regret, merely fondness for the ones I had left. My family was resigned to my being away. They no longer emphasized how much they missed me. They were eager to tell me their news. Father complained briefly that he had drilled two holes for a new well with no success. He was not bitter, and in fact he seemed accepting that a third, deeper hole would be required. "It's part of being a farmer," he told me. "Nothing comes easy."

The furies hid in the background of our lives.

Malignant Memory

Andy became more and more agitated as the end of July and the day of Great-Grandfather's arrival was imminent. She was increasingly vocal about her resentment toward her father. "He left us destitute. Because of him, my mother died. I went to the orphanage. And now I have to change my whole world just to look after him. It isn't fair." I listened and nodded, saying nothing.

Once I asked Andy what she remembered that was good about her father. She was pensive for several seconds. "Well, I guess I remember how when we were walking, all of a sudden, without any warning, he would jump right up in the air and start walking on fences. Tall fences, short fences, thin fences, picket fences. It didn't matter. He would make out like he was a circus performer walking on a tightrope. He would be grinning, acting like a silly clown. He never fell." She smiled at the memory.

"He sounds like fun," I said.

"He was," Andy replied reticently. "He was much more fun than my mother. She was strict. I think she had to be because he just wanted to be a kid. He never grew up. He loved to play games with us. Or invent special occasions. One of his favourites was a picnic in the living room. It was always a surprise. He would tell Mother that whatever she had cooked for lunch or supper could be thrown out because we were going to have a picnic instead. There would be a blanket and a picnic basket full of our favourite foods. Mother hated our picnics. We loved them, but then Mother had to clean up the mess after.

"Another thing I remember is that on the coldest winter days, the kind of day that is too cold to go outside, he would tell us girls, 'You know what we need today? Ice cream!' He'd get out the old ice cream maker. We'd turn the crank for hours until we had ice cream. It was the best ice cream I have ever had, sitting in our kitchen, eating ice cream while we looked outside at the snow and ice."

Andy stared into the distance. When she began again, her voice was soft, almost tender.

"I loved my father. I was crazy about him. I thought he loved us too. Then one day, without telling us what he was going to do, he left us. Everything went sour after that. We had no money. My baby brother was gone. My mother became ill. The last thing she said to me and my sisters was, 'Forgive your father.' Then I went into the orphanage."

Magnanimity

Suddenly Andy spoke with such vehemence that I backed away from her, afraid.

"I will never forgive him for what he did. Never. Never."

It was June, the end of the school year, before I realized I was no longer lonely. I basked in my new friendship with Hannah and the increasing comfort I experienced in Andy's home. I eagerly waited for my great-grandfather's arrival.

CHAPTER EIGHT

THE RECKONING

I crossed the days off the calendar until Great-Grandfather arrived from New York. I was excited, but I was fearful—afraid that the stress of having her hated father in the house would be a breaking point for Andy, that the furies would come back.

Andy was washing the windows in the living room two days before Great-Grandfather's arrival. I was reading in a wingback chair. Andy turned to face me. She spoke so quietly that at first I could not make out what she was saying. "Pardon me?"

"It is my fault that my father left us."

She paused then, turning to stare out the window. Her voice was strained, sad, when she began again.

"On the day he left, I was sick. I had a fever. I had scarlet fever. I was miserable. He was trying to cheer me up, make me feel better. He had bought me a china doll I named Betsy. I loved the doll, but I was cranky with my father. I told him I wanted him to stay home with me. I was his pet, you see. He usually did what I wanted.

"He said no at first, he had to go to work at the factory. Mother and my sister Helen had scarlet fever before me. My father had been away from work a lot that month. But I begged him to stay home with me. I cried. Finally, he agreed. He stayed home. We played together, tea parties and dolls, things like that.

"The factory foreman came to our house in the afternoon. He told Father he was fired. He yelled at Father that he was useless, a disgrace. My mother heard the foreman and she started to cry. She said we would be penniless. She said she couldn't live anymore

Malignant Memory

with all the stress. The baby started crying. All the commotion had woken him.

"Father kissed Mother on the cheek. Then he took the baby. He walked out the door. We thought he was taking the baby for a walk. We never saw him again. Or my baby brother."

I sat, waiting for her to continue. She turned to face me.

"It was my fault. Everything that happened—him leaving, my baby brother going, my mother dying, our family falling apart—all because I made him stay home that day."

I wanted desperately to assure Andy that it was not her fault. I was certain her father had made the decision to leave his family because he was overwhelmed with the circumstances of his life, not because of Andy. But I knew, even at my young age, that there are some insights you cannot grant another person. No matter what I said, Andy was not ready to acknowledge her father's responsibility for his leaving. She needed to believe that he would never have left her if she hadn't manipulated him to stay away from work.

The day of Great-Grandfather's arrival finally came. Brain and Crane arrived early in the morning to bring us to the train station. Brain brought a vase filled with pink peonies from Thelma's garden for Great-Grandfather's bedroom. Andy was tense, quiet. I was filled with excitement and trepidation.

We waited on the platform for half an hour. Other passengers disembarked. There was no sign of Great-Grandfather.

"He hasn't come," Andy declared peevishly, as if she were both relieved and disappointed.

"Will you recognize him? I asked her.

"I don't know," she replied tersely. "All I remember is what he looks like in my memory of him. That was long ago."

Andy's sister Maude had taken all the family photographs when their mother died. Andy rarely talked to Maude. Their relationship was distant, conflicted. Andy could not bring herself to ask Maude for some photos of her family.

We glimpsed him just as Crane had decided to see the conductor for an explanation of Great-Grandfather's absence. A middle-aged woman in a blue nurse's uniform was holding his elbow, helping him down the train steps. They moved slowly toward us on the platform.

The Reckoning

Andy sucked in her breath. She stared at him in disbelief. "It's him," she said, more to herself than to us. "It's really him."

The nurse held out her hand and introduced herself. "Hello, you must be the Andersons. I am Nurse Donovan. I looked after Mr. Birch for the past six months at Belvedere Hospital in New York. He's almost good as new again, but he doesn't speak. The doctors say they don't know why he isn't speaking. They just can't find a reason for it."

Andy stood staring at her father. Great-Grandfather did not look up from his downward glance. His posture was slumped. He was small, barely five feet. His eyes were pale blue. When he finally looked up for a few seconds, I saw that the right eye was clouded, milky. His shoulder-length, snow white hair was sparse, fine, and wispy. Tiny crops of hair formed in his ears and nostrils. Several wayward hairs stuck out at right angles from his thick white eyebrows. He was dressed in grey pants and a white linen shirt much too large for his slight frame. Great-Grandfather held onto his pants at the waist as if he feared they might fall to the ground.

The nurse saw me staring at Great-Grandfather's footwear, too large corduroy slippers. "I am sorry we couldn't find shoes to fit him," she said. "His clothes were so torn and frayed that we had to throw them away. We get donations of clothes in the hospital, but there were no shoes his size. The slippers were the best we could do. I know the clothes don't fit him well, either. He'll need new ones when he's settled."

The nurse handed Crane a package in a brown paper bag. "That's his pills, the medicine he receives. All the instructions are inside. He doesn't take much, considering his age. His blood pressure has been a problem, always a little higher than it should be. But it's controlled with the medication. None of the doctors can get over how healthy he is. He's a spry old thing, our Mr. Birch. He can outrun me! You'd never guess he was eighty-seven."

The nurse looked down at her watch. "I really should get going. I have a train to catch back to New York." She paused to kiss Great-Grandfather on the cheek. "You be good, now." She turned to us. "He's a sweetie, really he is. He is the happiest person I have met in a long time. He seems to enjoy everybody and everything. I wish there were more like him."

Malignant Memory

Andy snorted.

The nurse turned abruptly to board her train. She waved from the train steps.

Brain and Crane retrieved Great-Grandfather's luggage and started toward home. Andy did not move. She stared and stared at Great-Grandfather. "What are we going to do with him? How are we going to cope?" she asked aloud to no one in particular.

I approached Great-Grandfather and put my hand under his chin, lifting his face to meet mine. He barely reached my shoulder.

"I am Elizabeth, your great granddaughter. People call me Ba," I told him. "I am very glad you are here." Great-Grandfather smiled, tentatively at first and then broadly. He placed his left hand in mine and squeezed my fingers lightly.

"I think I will call you GG," I said. "It's a lot easier to say than Great-Grandfather." GG smiled. He reached up to hug me. I was struck by how skeleton-thin he was, how trusting he seemed. He seemed fragile, defenseless, more like a small, frightened child than my senior relative or a father who had abandoned his family.

"Come on GG," I said to him. "Let's take you to your new home." We walked, hand in hand, to Crane's car.

GG was dazed and agitated when we arrived at Andy's house. He would not look at Andy who was scowling at him. He seemed not to see Brain and Crane. Brain tried addressing him, "Mr. Birch, let's get you a cup of tea and something to eat. You must be hungry after that long journey." GG ignored her.

Crane asked, "Mr. Birch, are you hungry?" GG turned his head away and looked down the street as if planning his escape.

Andy stood by the car on the sidewalk and watched Brain and Crane try to convince GG to enter the house. She said nothing.

"GG, would you like something to eat? A cup of tea?" I asked him. GG nodded vigorously. He took my hand and smiled. It struck me that GG was not unlike one of my younger brothers. He needed to be safe, to feel loved, to belong.

"Let's all call him GG," I said to the others. "He doesn't seem to like Mr. Birch." GG nodded.

Crane brought GG's luggage into the house. I took GG by the hand and led him to his new bedroom. "Let's put away your things."

The Reckoning

The contents of GG's luggage consisted of several books, a pair of eyeglasses broken at the nose piece, a denture cup, and a stained pair of red plaid boxer shorts. The books were my great-grandmother's. Her signature was on the inside of the front covers. One of the books was an early edition of Sonnets from the Portuguese.

Andy looked through the books. She looked puzzled, miffed. "My mother was a reader, just like you. She read all the time. My father couldn't read or write. I don't know why he has her books or how he got them."

Andy spied GG's pitiful possessions. She gazed up at the ceiling, loudly feigning supplication to God. "Don't tell me that I am going to have to buy him new clothes on top of everything else? Oh Lord, why me? Isn't it bad enough I have to look after him, give him a home, when he did neither for me? Do I have to go to the poor house for him too?" I watched her cheek muscles twitch.

GG cowered behind me. He whimpered. Andy scared him.

I put my arms around GG in a consoling hug. "It's Andy, your daughter, Henrietta." He hid his face in my shoulder. "Don't worry," I whispered, "She's very nice when you get to know her. She just needs time."

Andy stared at us for a few minutes and then left the room abruptly.

Crane suggested that he buy GG a pair of shoes. "I could trace his feet on a piece of paper," he told me. "I could bring the tracing to the shoe store and see what we could find."

"Shoes would be good," I replied. "We can get GG some more clothes tomorrow."

Crane traced GG's feet and then left to find shoes. He returned within the hour with a pair of brown loafers. GG was delighted. He clapped his hands and grinned broadly when Crane showed him the purchase. The shoes were a perfect fit. GG amused us for several minutes by putting on one shoe, taking it off and then putting on the other shoe. Finally, with both shoes on his feet, he walked proudly through the house, stopping periodically to admire his new footwear.

As the day continued, GG shadowed me everywhere I went. When I went to the bathroom, he followed me. "Not here," I told him firmly. "You need to give me some privacy." I opened the door when I was finished on the toilet. GG fell to the floor, bumping his head. "He's been standing against the door, waiting for you, since you went in," Andy told me.

Malignant Memory

The next day, Andy and I took GG to get his hair cut, have his eyeglasses repaired, and buy him new clothes. He was so thin and short that we had trouble fitting men's clothes to his frame. The sales clerk suggested we try clothes for boys. Soon we had outfitted GG with two pullover sweaters, underwear, socks, three pairs of trousers, and five shirts. "Isn't this expensive?" I asked Andy. "Don't worry about it," she replied. "My sisters sent guilt money. It's enough to pay for the clothes, and then my sisters won't feel bad about ditching the old man on us."

GG looked like a new man when we returned home. His hair was cut short. His ears, nose, and eyebrows had been trimmed. He was wearing clothes that showed off his tiny but muscular frame. His glasses had been repaired, and a new, more stylish pair had been ordered.

"You have pretty eyes," I told him. "I can see them so much better with your haircut and your new blue shirt." GG smiled as he caught his reflection in the hallway mirror.

We soon established a routine together. Andy stayed out of our way. GG stayed with me wherever I went.

I had thought that GG would tolerate being left with others or being alone as he felt more comfortable with us, but he continued to follow me everywhere I went even after several days had passed. He became agitated and anxious when I left his sight even for a few minutes. "He's like a devoted puppy," Brain declared when I took GG to the library.

Most of the time, I enjoyed his company. He did not demand much and required little. GG was simply content to be in my presence. I never saw him cranky or irritated. The simplest things delighted him. He would clap his hands with glee if I gave him a photograph album to look at or if he saw a bird at the feeder. He smiled almost all the time.

GG would squat on my bedroom floor as I wrote letters to my family, waiting quietly until I took him to the library or to Brain and Crane's house. We would swing side-by-side at the park until I said it was time to go. While I was occupied with other things, he would spend several minutes making the veins in his hands dance by contracting the muscles in his hands. Thanks to a new pair of glasses, he could see images much better than when he first arrived. He could not read, but he loved looking at pictures in books. He would thumb through the same books for hours at a time.

The Reckoning

One of GG's favourite pastimes was to look through the roll-top desk for secret compartments. He delighted in finding drawers within drawers, false bottoms of drawers, and drawers that seemed to be part of the desk's finishing. He located twelve of these secret compartments in all. He placed memories—a bird feather, a fallen button—in each one. He would spend time each day finding the artifacts he had stored and then replacing them once again in their mysterious location.

GG's energy was astounding for someone who was 87. He could put on his socks with his leg straight out, perpendicular to the floor, standing on one foot. Once he tried to climb a giant oak tree in the cemetery. He was halfway up the tree when I noticed. I had to scream at him before he shimmied down to the ground. I was frantic that he might fall. When he was on level ground again, he simply kissed me on the cheek and grinned widely. "You are a scamp," I said, pretending to be cross. GG laughed delightedly.

I would often wake in the night to discover GG sitting cross-legged at the side of my bed. "What do you want?" I would ask him. I did not conceal my irritation at his invasion of my private space. He would reach out to stroke my cheek or give me a kiss on my arm. Then he would leave to return to his bed. I would be awake in my bed, wondering what he wanted, what he was thinking about, why he never spoke.

Andy suggested that we lock my bedroom door at night. "You need to get your sleep, and that old man should not be in a young girl's bedroom," she declared passionately.

The next night, the bedroom door was locked. GG sat on the floor by the door, whimpering and knocking until I could no longer stand it. "Please let him come in," I begged Andy. "He just wants to see me. He'll go back to his bed once he knows I am okay." Andy reluctantly agreed. "We'll never get any sleep if we don't let him in."

There were times when I craved time alone, when I reminisced with fondness about when Andy and I could decide to go somewhere without having to consider another person. GG was little trouble. Other than at night, he seemed to know intuitively when I was not to be disturbed. He never pulled at my sleeve when I was reading, nor was he irritating in any way. Still, he was someone that needed care. Sometimes I didn't want to be GG's caregiver.

GG did not speak, but he understood everything we said to him.

Malignant Memory

He had novel, creative ways of communicating with me through gestures and imitations. Once he flapped his arms and walked like a bird to let me know that a redheaded woodpecker was in our backyard. His pantomime of Andy caring for our neighbour was so accurate that it made me giggle. I understood his message, Why is she so preoccupied with others' needs and yet she overlooks her own?

GG ignored Andy most of the time, but if she spoke softly, he would respond to her requests. Andy feigned kindness and affection, hoping that GG would be less afraid of her, but he preferred to stay as far away from Andy as possible.

GG soon began to relate to Brain. Brain greeted GG with a hug each time she saw him. He leaned into her hugs as if he craved them. She brought him books from the library that had particularly appealing photos of animals, travel, and people. Soon, if I wanted to spend time alone in the library stacks, I would tell him to sit with Brain. She would motion for him to sit in a chair beside her. She would chatter to him about the events of the day until I returned.

Crane developed a rapport with GG simply by being near him, by being as silent as GG himself. One day, Crane and GG were sitting at the library table, Crane reading and GG looking at pictures in books. Brain called over to Crane. She wanted him to fetch something from the third floor. Crane pushed his chair away from the table and stood. GG put his hand in Crane's. They walked together to find what Brain needed. After that, GG was as content to spend time with Crane as he was with Brain and me.

Once, GG saw a photo in a book of an orangutan imitating the photographer. He laughed out loud, startling us with the noise. "I was going to tell him that he needed to be quiet in the library," Brain told me later, "but it was so lovely to hear him make a happy sound. I didn't bother."

GG laughed and grinned when he played with Brain and Crane's dogs. When I told this to Andy, she smiled, "I had forgotten that about him. He loved animals, especially dogs, when we were young. They would follow him wherever he went. We had many dogs in our home."

Hannah visited our home often. GG loved her from the first time he saw her. She had an instinctive way of making GG feel comfortable around her. GG and Hannah would sit for hours, looking at pictures of dogs together. Hannah would make funny comments about the dogs.

The Reckoning

"Can you imagine how much it would cost to feed a dog like that?" You would have to wear a raincoat to protect yourself from all its slobber." GG would laugh and laugh.

Hannah told me, "I have so much trouble seeing GG as the evil man who left his family. He is so sweet, so gentle." I nodded in agreement.

It was late August. School would begin again in a few weeks. Andy and I were sitting at the table, finishing supper. GG was looking at pictures in a book in the living room. I broached the subject of GG's care when I was away at school.

"What are we going to do?" I asked her. "He hates it if I am not with him. He has to know that I am around."

Andy was petulant. "You can't take him to school. Brain and Crane can't look after him in the library. He'll just have to put up with me."

She added sharply, "Not that it'll be a picnic for me to have him around all day. I can barely stand the sight of him. I hate him." I cringed thinking of sweet GG being with Andy who despised him. I wanted to object, to tell her that GG was no trouble, but I kept quiet. I knew that she would not be open to thinking of GG in positive ways.

I talked to Brain about my dilemma. "The thing is," I told her, "GG is really very sweet. I couldn't bear it if Andy were to have the furies with him when I was at school. How would he be able to protect himself?"

Brain came up with a plan. "We have three weeks before school begins," she said confidently. "Let's start getting GG used to you being away gradually, a little bit at a time. He'll be with Andy for just a few minutes at first and then we'll gradually increase the time until they are used to spending whole days together." She paused, and then said solemnly, "Andy hasn't had the furies for a few months now. I think she'll be fine with GG."

I was not convinced. I had observed Andy becoming tenser around GG. I was not at all confident that Andy B wouldn't make an appearance if I was away.

Andy agreed to the plan only because she could not think of an alternative. The next day I told GG, "I am going out for a few minutes. Andy is here. She'll look after you." GG started to whimper. He clung to me. I forced myself to push him away. "You will be fine," I told him. I turned and went out the door. I hid around the corner of the house.

GG's whimpers soon became outright cries. He was hollering, wailing. Andy's voice was angry and loud. "Shut up, shut up. You have to stay with me. I don't want you either, but we have to be together until Ba comes back." I rushed back into the house. GG's face was wet with tears. He ran to me with his arms outstretched. Andy's face was flushed, her cheek muscles danced their ominous jig.

It took more than an hour for GG to let me go. He clung to me, his arms wrapped tightly around my waist. Andy retreated to her bedroom, slamming the door behind her.

I increased the length of my absences each day. By the second week, I was out of the house for 30 minutes. GG's hysteria and Andy's anger escalated with each absence. "I don't think this is working," I told Brain. "They hate each other."

Brain suggested that perhaps Andy and GG knew I was merely hiding nearby. "They know you haven't really gone away. Maybe it's time to go somewhere else, somewhere far from the house. Then they will be forced to face one another. They will be forced to work it out."

The next day, I went to Hannah's house down the street. I returned in 45 minutes. I could hear Andy's piercing screams as I walked up to the front door. It was the voice of the furies.

"You miserable excuse for a man, you destroyed us all. You killed my mother, you made me go to the orphanage, you took my brother. Where is my brother, you horrible man? Where? Where?"

I ran up the steps to open the door. Andy was bent over GG's prostrate form on the carpet. She was beating him with her fists.

I summoned all the courage I could muster. I had a book in my hand. I shoved it in Andy's face, touching her nose with the book. "Stop!" I screamed as loud as I could. "Stop hitting him."

Andy was startled. She stepped back from GG, her mouth hung open and slack in shock. She slowly lowered her hands to her sides.

"Go into your bedroom," I commanded her. I was surprised by the authority in my voice. I was in charge now. I was not going to allow Andy B to hurt GG.

"I will look after GG. You wait in your room until I come for you."

Andy slunk to her bedroom. She did not look back at us.

I gathered GG in my arms and consoled him the best that I could. He was sobbing. His skin had been scratched at his temple and above his elbow. He had a bruise forming above his left eye. I bandaged him, all the while explaining to him about the furies. I told him that I would teach him

The Reckoning

how to make Andy B cower, how to stop her assault. I was not at all certain that I knew how he could do this, but I assured him we would find a way.

GG lay his head on my chest and blubbered for a long time. At last, he was so spent by the experience that he fell asleep. I lay him gently on the living room couch and placed a blanket over him. He snored peacefully.

I knocked on Andy's door. She stood in the doorway sheepish and contrite. She too looked exhausted.

"You had the furies again." My voice was tremulous. My legs were shaking with the rage that consumed me. "This can never happen again. GG is too frail. You could have killed him. You have to find a way to live with him."

Andy nodded. She stared dejectedly at her shoes.

"I am going to get you help," I told her. "From Brain and Thelma." I started down the hallway, away from her. "We need to fix this." I added more gently, "You rest for now. We'll find a way to fix this."

I telephoned Brain and told her what had happened. "Crane will get Thelma," she said. "We'll bring Thelma to your house."

I sighed with relief. Thelma would help us. Thelma would fix us.

CHAPTER NINE

MIRACLES

Thelma slowly manoeuvered her large, awkward frame up Andy's front steps with the help of her cane, Crane's arm, and fierce determination. Crane helped her to find a seat on one of the wingback chairs. The chair groaned and swayed with her weight. "I am staying," Thelma declared. "I am staying here until GG can be safe with Andy."

I moved Thelma's luggage to my bedroom. I took my belongings to my former room. I stared at the uncomfortable cot and the windowless walls, already regretting the move. "Never mind," I told myself. "If Thelma can make it so Andy and GG can live together peacefully, it'll all be worth it."

Brain and Crane left us to return to the library. I made supper. Andy joined us at the table. She ate nothing and said little. She did not look directly at Thelma or me. I woke GG, but he was not hungry. He went to his bed and stayed there until the next morning.

Thelma talked brightly to us at the dinner table. She spoke of her garden, her grandchildren, funny things she had heard, and the predictions for weather. No one mentioned the furies.

The following morning, GG noticed Thelma. It was instant love. He adored her. He followed her everywhere she went. I was resentful. GG had never showed such dedication to anyone but me before. He liked Hannah, and Brain and Crane, but this level of devotion had previously been mine alone.

Thelma smiled at me, "Don't be jealous, little one. GG knows that you share something with him that few others do. GG knows we are kindred spirits."

Malignant Memory

I went to see Brain at the library the next morning. "Stay away all morning, at least four hours," Thelma advised. "It'll give me time to discover things about this situation." She did not elaborate on what the "things" might be.

Brain asked me how things were at home. I confessed that I felt nervous, anxious, about what might be happening in my absence. I remembered Andy's assault on GG and shuddered. "I wish I could stay with him," I told Brain. "But Thelma said I had to leave. I hope he'll be all right."

Brain listened. She gave no advice nor offered false assurances. "This must be so hard for you," she said gently. "Two people you love and they are both hurting."

I was startled by her words. I knew I loved GG. Who wouldn't love that sweet man? And of course I was worried about his welfare when Andy was vindictive. But I had never acknowledged that I loved Andy before. And then I knew with a certainty that caught my breath that it was Andy's pain that was my greatest concern. She was having to relive her father's abandonment and to experience shame for having the furies again. I was filled with compassion for my grandmother.

Thelma, GG, and Andy were sitting on the living room floor when I returned from the library. "We're having a picnic," Thelma said. "Andy went to the store to get us some picnic food. GG put a blanket on the floor. I got us some lemonade from the fridge. There's a place for you at our picnic. Sit down and join us."

I looked at the three adults and smiled. GG was beaming with happiness. Thelma's massive frame was propped by many pillows. She was grinning. Andy was not smiling but neither was she tense. She seemed surprisingly content.

I enjoyed the picnic. GG and I laughed uproariously when Thelma told us that Andy had refused to swim at Thelma's lake because she had watched the movie "African Queen." She became convinced that piranhas would bite off her toes if she swam. Thelma said, "There was no convincing her that piranhas don't live in the lake. It was a good five years before she would swim in that water."

Andy grinned widely, recalling her unreasonable fear of Thelma's lake. "I eventually swam with the others, but my toes would cramp up something terrible whenever I swam. I never told them. I was trying to keep them curled up tight so the piranhas wouldn't get them."

Miracles

Andy surprised me later by saying, "This has been fun. Let's have a picnic in the living room again some time." GG stared at her thoughtfully.

Over time, Thelma helped us to discover new ways for GG and Andy to relate to us. One day she announced, "You need a dog. Ba says that GG loves dogs. A dog would be good for you both." Andy balked at the idea at first. She told Thelma she had not had a pet since she was a child. She protested that dogs were messy and smelly. She objected to the expense of dog food. She said that she had no experience training a dog. She said she couldn't rely on GG to help care for the dog.

She said categorically, "No dog. No way."

Thelma remained resolute.

The week before I was to begin grade eleven, Andy capitulated. She agreed to go to the pound to find a dog. GG clapped his hands and danced a little jig in his delight at this pronouncement.

It was a strange-looking dog that Andy rescued from the pound. Thelma declared that the dog was God's idea of a joke. The mutt was an amalgam of several dog breeds packaged together to form a strange, awkward creature unlike any dog I had ever seen. It had the long narrow snout of a Dachshund, the short stubby legs of a Basset Hound, the tall lean body of a Dalmatian, and the thick muscular tail of a Golden Retriever. Her nose was pink.

The dog had wiry, stiff grey hair that stood straight and unyielding. It could not be smoothed, nor could it be brushed to lie flat. "She looks like a walking scrub brush," Thelma declared, laughing.

Andy explained that she had chosen the dog because the man at the pound had told her that no one wanted her. "He said that people thought she was funny looking, ugly. They didn't want her. But the man said she was the sweetest dog. She has a very friendly disposition. She loves to be with people. She rarely barks. She is very loving." Andy paused and then added. "I know what it feels like to not be wanted, so I chose this dog. Any objections?" She looked at us defiantly. We said nothing.

GG could not contain his joy. He crawled on his hands and knees to meet the dog. He patted her tenderly, looking into her eyes as she licked his face. Andy grinned, nodding happily as she watched her father and the dog play together. Soon the dog lay on Andy's feet, curled in a ball. She was sleeping. Andy did not move a muscle until the dog woke and went to her water bowl.

Malignant Memory

I mentioned the dog's arrival in my weekly phone call to my family. Mother was flabbergasted. "Andy, your grandmother, let you have a dog? I can't believe it. She wouldn't let your father have any pet, even a goldfish, when he was young. She always thought dogs were dirty. I have to see this with my own eyes to believe it. Andy and a dog! Amazing!"

Andy told us, "We'll have to find a name for our dog. It's not right for her not to have a name. I'll say some names and you tell me if you like them." I started to suggest names. Thelma motioned for me to join her in the kitchen. "You have to let them have the dog together," Thelma whispered. "They will love the dog, and in that love they will discover their love for each other." I was indignant. I was very fond of dogs. I wanted to be part of the dog's life too. But Thelma's advice had always been correct. I stayed out of the conversation.

GG and Andy settled on "Aphrodite" as the dog's name. "We decided to name her after the Greek goddess of love and beauty because her beauty is the way she loves," Andy told us. Thelma and I stared at the world's ugliest dog. We said nothing.

Just as the man at the pound had promised, Aphrodite was a sweet-natured, loving dog. We all fell in love with her. Aphrodite seemed to know instinctively when we were not feeling well or when we were sad or unhappy. Once when Thelma's arthritis was plaguing her with pain, Aphrodite spent the day at Thelma's side, her head resting in Thelma's lap, looking up at Thelma with compassion. Thelma said it was the best therapy she had ever encountered.

It was great fun having Thelma in our house. She told stories about her ancestors, legends about the creation of the world, parables involving animals, and stories from her past. She laughed freely and often. Andy joined her in the laughter. They were close friends. It was good to see Andy so relaxed and content.

I began grade eleven happier and more confident than when I had first arrived in Kingsford. I no longer felt like a newcomer to the school. I had a friend now. Some of the teachers had been impressed with my abilities the previous year. They offered me opportunities to get involved in new learning challenges. I joined the drama club, a club that mimicked federal politics, and another club that examined international issues. I grew as a person and a thinker.

I was more comfortable with Catholicism in my second year of high school. I no longer needed justification from the nuns for what they believed. I had read about enough different faiths in the library to know that none were without their contradictions or peculiarities. I decided to appreciate the many beautiful things about the Catholic tradition and overlook the rest. I took what I appreciated about Catholicism and added these to the articles of faith I had learned to value in Buddhism, Hinduism, Judaism, Protestantism, and Islam. It was a recipe of my own design for "living in faith."

Because I no longer questioned them, the nuns believed that I had experienced a conversion to Catholicism over the summer. They often used me as the exemplar of true faith to other students. "She used to be sceptical about our faith, a non-believer, and now she is a believer."

Grade eleven was my introduction to Sister Margaret Rose. She had been ill, away from the school for the first two weeks of the school year. Her English literature class was taught by a tightly wound woman, Mamie Mills, who found all adolescents irritating. Miss Mills made each of us take turns reading Silas Marner aloud. She never commented on the book or invited our comments about it. She was merely filling in time until the actual teacher, Sister Margaret Rose, returned. I struggled to stay focussed during the tortured readings. Many of my classmates fell asleep. To this day, I cannot hear about Silas Marner without feeling a need for a nap.

Sister Margaret Rose entered our classroom one fateful day in September. She was a mountain of a woman, six feet tall and almost as wide. She was grinning from ear to ear, seemingly thrilled to be in our presence. She glanced at the roll call on her desk and threw it aside. "Now," she announced. "Let's get to know one another." She invited us to ask her any question we liked. The deal she made was she would answer any question we posed, but then she could in turn ask us something.

The irascible Hannah Austin was the first to give her a question to answer. "Did you ever have sex with a man?" The class gasped in disbelief. Even for Hannah, this question was out of line.

Sister Margaret Rose was calm, even nonchalant in her response. "No I haven't," she said smiling. "I wasn't too popular with the boys before I went into the convent. I liked boys. For a while, I even fantasized sometimes about marrying one. But they didn't like me as a girlfriend. I was taller than most of them, wider than all of them. Most men were afraid they would not survive an encounter with me." She laughed delightedly.

Malignant Memory

Her question to Hannah was, "Who do you most admire and why?"

Hannah was eager to answer. She told Sister Margaret Rose that the person she most admired was her mother. She spoke passionately about how her mother had inspired in her a love of good books and critical thought. I had met Hannah's mother only once when Andy and I had visited her home. Hannah's mother had not spoken much at all. Mostly she slept on the couch, looking deathly ill. It was hard to imagine her as inspirational.

Hannah went on to tell Sister Margaret Rose that her mother had been abandoned by Hannah's father. She said, "The weird thing is that my father did this to her. He left her without any money, nothing. And she's Catholic so divorce and remarriage is out of the question. But people treat my mother as if she was the one who did something wrong. Most of our neighbours look down on her. They blame her because he left, because we are poor. They say cruel things to her."

I watched, my mouth open in disbelief. Hannah never spoke about her mother's abandonment or their poverty. Not even to me.

Sister Margaret Rose listened intently. She said, "That's not fair is it? We are going to be reading Hardy's Tess of the D'Urbervilles later this month. Maybe you have already read it?" Hannah shook her head. "Well, you will see that Tess too is blamed for the sins of others even though she was the victim. It's an old book, but it is entirely relevant to today. There were double standards then and there are double standards in existence today. I am looking forward to hearing what you think of the book."

Hannah smiled. I had never before seen her smile without disdain at a teacher.

Soon other students began to ask Sister Margaret Rose questions. They asked her about her life before and after the convent, her experiences as a teacher, her taste in music, her talents, and her faults. She answered each question openly. She laughed often, as much at herself as the rest of us. She asked us questions about what we read, what we found interesting and what we found dull in life, and our personal goals. The two-hour-long class was animated, entertaining, and compelling. We did not discuss English literature, but we were eager to learn what Sister Margaret Rose would teach us.

Just as we suspected in our first meeting with her, Sister Margaret Rose was an engaging, gifted teacher. She was a welcome relief from the taciturn Miss Mills.

Miracles

We loved going to her class. We not only learned and grew as thinkers, we also had fun.

Sister Margaret Rose began every class with a new joke. We waited for it eagerly. "There was a travelling salesman who was driving along a country road. Suddenly, he heard a terrible thump. He got out of his car to look. He had killed a little rabbit! The man was mortified. Suddenly, a farmer appeared. He told the salesman not to worry. He poured some liquid from a bottle onto the rabbit's head. The rabbit immediately got up and starting hopping away. The rabbit stopped every few minutes to turn to the farmer and wave his paw. The salesman was overcome. 'What magic was in that bottle?' he asked the farmer. The farmer replied, 'Hair restorer with permanent wave.'"

Her jokes were corny. We often groaned out loud when she got to the punchline. I still remember some of those jokes this many years later. Sister Margaret Rose had dimples on each cheek. Her dimples accentuated her expressions of delight whenever she read aloud a passage she particularly admired, or when we contributed a comment that she thought was inspired. Making Sister Margaret Rose's dimples appear soon became every student's goal.

Sister Margaret Rose made what we read come alive. She acted out scenes from books as if she were auditioning for the stage. She read poems to us as if the words were her own, wrought from the joys and agonies of her life's experiences. She tied our assigned reading to our real lives. "That's not just a story from long ago," she was prone to remarking, "The author wanted to teach you something that you could use in your lifetime. If you don't connect to what the author wants to tell you, maybe you haven't tried hard enough. Or maybe you haven't lived enough to understand."

In Sister Margaret Rose's class, no idea was rejected, no opinions were privileged. Sister Margaret Rose's only commandment was "think critically and think well." I was thrilled with the level of the discussion and the freedom to say whatever I thought.

Sister Margaret Rose did not follow the curriculum established at St. Theresa's for English literature. A student once asked her if we would be reading about the lives of the saints. She said, "My older sister said that's what we read in this class." Sister Margaret Rose stared at the girl for a few seconds before she answered. "If you want to read about the lives of the saints, by all means read about them. I can even give you a couple of books on the topic. But in this class, I want to prepare you for the real world. I want to hone your thinking skills, to help you to be ready for the decisions you will face when you are no longer living at home with your parents." She turned to face the entire class. "You will not all see the books I assign in the same way. You will have different interpretations of the passages we study. The books I assign are designed to challenge your thinking, to help you to articulate what it is that you think and believe. That is critical to your success as an adult, as a woman."

    Sister Margaret Rose's first assigned reading was Aldous Huxley's essay on time. Our class debated the meaning of the essay in class and for many days afterward, in the school cafeteria and in each other's homes after school.

    Sister Margaret Rose told wonderfully vivid stories about her life before the convent. Once she told us that her father had run a women's dress shop in Ontario. There was a group of dresses he could not sell. He reduced the price of the dresses several times. Each time, no one purchased a dress. He even reduced the price to below his cost. Still the dresses remained on the rack, unsold. He took the dresses to the storeroom. He left them in the storeroom for a year. Then he placed the dresses back in the store. He marked them with prices higher than any other dress in the store. The dresses sold in two days. Sister Margaret Rose assigned us an essay. She said, "Take the story I told you and make sense of it by drawing on the ideas in Ayn Rand's *Atlas Shrugged*." It was typical of the assignments in Sister Margaret Rose's class in that it challenged me to read the novel with a critical eye, to claim my thoughts, and to relate my reading to the real world of human behaviour.

    Sister Margaret Rose was kind and affirming in her feedback to us about our assignments. "Great job! I loved the way you questioned the way the author ended her novel." "You were so right about the allegory of the storm and the author's illness. Good for you for finding out a bit of the poet's life history that helps make sense of why she used this allegory." She did not, however, compromise on her expectations of us to be committed learners.

    Once, Sister Margaret Rose gave each of us a piece of paper on which she had written a sentence from Shakespeare's play *Hamlet*. She told us to write an essay about how that sentence related to our lives. My paper contained a line spoken by Ophelia: "And there are pansies, they're for thoughts."

There were far better quotes from Hamlet that she could have given me. "To be or not to be," would have been an amazing sentence to write about. I had never cared for Ophelia as a character. She was too weak-kneed, too spineless, for my liking. She chose suicide rather than to disobey her parents or to confront Hamlet. I was angry, petulant, when I wrote the essay.

I wrote the essay in less than an hour. I wrote that Ophelia taught me to obey my parents, to remain steadfast to the rules of the church and my teachers. I said that if she had been able to talk to Hamlet, to tell him that she loved him but was torn between him and her parents, all would have been well. I wrote that communication is critical in life.

I was shocked speechless when I looked at the corrected paper. I was used to Sister Margaret Rose telling me that my work was outstanding. I was not prepared for the red F that marked the first page of my essay.

She wrote in the margins, "This essay is very disappointing. I chose the passage I gave you deliberately. I thought you would be capable of arriving at some sense of what Shakespeare intended. I thought you would be able to see that it is an insightful sentence that reveals the terrible circumstances of a woman in Ophelia's situation. I was wrong. What you have written in this essay is superficial. You have been given many gifts. You are clever and a good writer. You are capable of much more than what you have done in this essay. You have squandered your talents. I am giving you an F.

"If you wish, you can rewrite this paper. I will give you two days. If you hand in another version of the essay by Friday of this week, I will mark it. If the mark is better than an F, I will enter the new mark as the one you achieved for this assignment."

I was furious. I would not look at Sister Margaret Rose. I did not engage in the class discussion that day. I complained about Sister Margaret Rose to Andy later that day. "She's mean. Unfair. Betty Preston got a B. I read her essay. It wasn't any better than mine. And she got a much easier passage to write about."

Andy listened to my diatribe thoughtfully. Her only response was, "You better get writing."

I spent most of the first evening cultivating my sense of injustice about the wrong that had been done to me. "It's not fair! I deserve an A, not an F." It was only on the second day that I began to delve into the meaning of the words spoken by Ophelia; "And there are pansies, they're for thoughts." I re-read the play in its entirety.

It was early Friday morning, in the hours before dawn, that I suddenly understood. Ophelia is talking about what she keeps hidden from others about what she is thinking. She is referring to who she is and who she pretends to be. She is speaking about the tortuous battle she is experiencing between her two selves, one visible to others and the other hidden from view.

I began writing, slowly at first and then frantically, as if the remaining time would never be sufficient to explore the depths of Ophelia's statement. The words flowed onto the paper freely, without censure or constraint.

I wrote about how little we know of the true nature of people; how little we are able to fully interpret why people respond the way they do or act in the way in which they do. I wrote about how rarely our judgments of people are based on the full knowledge of their histories or their true identities. I gave examples from my own life that substantiated these claims. I related times in which my true motivations and intentions were hidden even from myself until some incident revealed them. I concluded the essay with several paragraphs about how the resolution between the two halves of ourselves, the hidden and the visible, is the only sustainable path to personal peace, how it is the secrets in our lives that will ultimately destroy us if we allow them to be hidden from others.

When I submitted the essay to Sister Margaret Rose on Friday morning, I no longer cared about the grade she would give me. I had learned a great deal. I had grown in the experience.

Sister Margaret Rose's written feedback was succinct. "This is a paper worthy of your gifts. A+."

Our class became fiercely loyal to Sister Margaret Rose. She had our unquestioned loyalty. We were her greatest publicists. We were vocal about her talents as a teacher and her goodness. Hannah said that if Sister Margaret Rose told us to jump off the Kingsford bridge, we would be fighting for first place at the jump off spot.

Our other teachers began to make subtle and not-so-subtle inferences that Sister Margaret Rose was not the great person we thought

Miracles

her to be. They began to complain that we were always talking about her. A lay teacher said, "Girls, if I hear one more thing about how wonderful Sister Margaret Rose is, I am going to scream!"

One afternoon, Sister Margaret Rose addressed the class. She was sad, distracted when she spoke.

"I need to correct my teaching practices." She paused, collecting her thoughts. "It seems as if it is not right that I provide an experience for you that is not traditional in the school. I shouldn't deviate from the curriculum. I should treat all students the same. I should no longer encourage hilarity." She spoke mechanically, as if she was merely repeating what someone had told her to say.

Hannah hissed, "It's that bloody Sister Agnes and her allies. They're just jealous. They hate that you are so popular as a teacher, Sister Margaret Rose. That you are so good at what you do."

Hannah crossed her arms defiantly across her chest. "We'll fight them."

The other students offered their protests.

"They can't do this. We won't let them."

"How dare they do this? We will demand that they let you continue."

"It's so unfair. We are learning so much."

"It's terrible. This class was the only thing I looked forward to. I feel like going to public school now."

I sat quietly. I felt powerless. I watched Sister Margaret Rose's shoulders slump. She whispered, "You needn't stop learning, just because my teaching will have changed. You can always read more than what we talk about in class. You can discuss what you read with each other after school. I need to confine my teaching to the curriculum."

Sister Margaret Rose had been instructed to stick religiously to the highly structured and monotonous curriculum. She seemed to have lost her fervour for teaching. I missed Sister Margaret Rose's exuberant and passionate teaching more than I can describe. The English literature class was not the same. She told us what to think about what we read; she did not ask what we thought. She required us to memorize answers about the books and poems she assigned so that we could attain the highest grades on exams.

The only positive outcome of what came to be known as the "Blackballing of Sister Margaret Rose" was that my friendship with the obstinate, outspoken Hannah was cemented.

Malignant Memory

Hannah could not forget what Sister Agnes and the others had done to squash Sister Margaret Rose's creativity and passion in the classroom. She delighted in discovering ways to humiliate the other teachers and to point out that Sister Margaret Rose was superior to them in every way.

Hannah had an uncanny knack of knowing when a teacher lacked confidence in what she was teaching. Her photographic memory catalogued facts and arguments from her voracious reading. She used these to annihilate a teacher's confidence with swift and deadly accuracy.

When Sister Ruth, an outspoken critic of Sister Margaret Rose, said that Darwin's theory of evolution was wrong, Hannah asked her why. Sister Ruth blushed. Sister Ruth had encountered Hannah's acerbic tongue before. She stammered, "Because the Pope said it was." The rest of us cringed, waiting for Hannah's attack. Hannah spoke quickly for over 20 minutes, showering Sister Ruth with arguments and facts. She gave numerous examples of where Popes had erred and how evolution was justified. She ended with, "And if you weren't a complete idiot, you would know that."

Once, our history teacher, another of Sister Margaret Rose's enemies, announced to us, "If it weren't for us winning the War of 1812, there wouldn't be a Canada today. We'd all be Americans." Hannah put up her hand. The teacher ignored her; all the teachers knew that when Hannah spoke, their reputations would be sullied. Hannah interrupted the teacher. The teacher tried vainly to silence Hannah, drawing on her authority to do so. "Students do not speak in this class unless I give permission for them to do so."

Hannah grinned widely. She popped a piece of gum in her mouth, an act strictly forbidden at St. Theresa's, and chewed it in an exaggerated loud motion. She leaned back in her seat, gazing at the increasingly discomforted teacher with disdain. She spoke over the teacher's objections.

"People weren't Canadians in 1812. In fact, the typical citizen in Upper Canada was an American who had come to this country because of the cheap land and low taxes." Hannah continued her tirade, peppering it with facts about the perplexing War of 1812, until the teacher finally sat down at her desk in defeat. Hannah ended her lesson with, "Really, I would have expected more from you as a teacher. We can always trust what Sister Margaret Rose says in her class. But you seem to not know

Miracles

your subject as well as she knows hers."

Hannah had more detentions and suspensions at St. Theresa's than any student before or since.

It occurs to me now that Hannah's campaign to reveal the injustice of what had happened to Sister Margaret Rose must have backfired. Surely the other teachers resented Sister Margaret Rose even more after Hannah's merciless attacks on their competence. But I admired Hannah, not only for her commitment to my favourite teacher, but also her incredible assurance and her unwavering commitment to righting a wrong.

I respected Hannah's bravery, her ability to say what she was thinking with no apparent care for how others' evaluated her. I envied her ability to live an undivided life. She was funny, quick-witted, and preposterous. I thought she was the most interesting person of my age that I had ever met.

Hannah would often entertain Andy, GG, and me, relating things she had read or what she thought about current events. One of her favourite topics was why people are often silent, even complacent, when great wrongs are done to other people.

Andy and GG loved listening to Hannah. They were pleased when she visited. This was surprising because Andy was vehement that she did not allow profanity in her home. Hannah used profanity constantly and masterfully to emphasize her views. "Fucking shitheads" and "Shit-filled dicks" were two of her favourite descriptors of people she disagreed with.

Brain and Crane joined us for supper with Hannah some nights. Brain loved to debate with Hannah; they were equally matched combatants, engaged as much in the process of argument as they were in what they were debating. Crane watched them silently, contributing little to the discussion.

Crane whispered to me one night as Hannah was leaving, "She reminds me of a firecracker that gives one dramatic, beautiful display of fireworks before it fizzles out. I hope that the passion she has will not burn her out."

It was Hannah who told me the first secret in high school. Hannah was pregnant. The father was a university student who frequented the restaurant in which Hannah worked on weekends.

Malignant Memory

The boy had accosted her in the alley as she was leaving the restaurant to return home after her shift. He pushed her down in the gravel. He raped her.

"I thought he liked me. He told me I was so much more intelligent than the other girls he knows."

It was unnerving to see the invincible Hannah mew like a frightened kitten. It scared me.

Hannah begged me not to tell anyone about the rape. She said the news would kill her mother. "She wanted me to go to university," Hannah sobbed.

Hannah said it was useless to go to the police. "It will be his word against mine. They all think I am weird. He's a university student. He is from a good family. They will think I am lying. Maybe I'll get an abortion."

Abortions were illegal back then. I had heard stories of girls being butchered by abortionists. My thoughts were frantic, jumbled. Would she be able to have more children after the abortion? Would she be discovered and imprisoned? Would she be sentenced to hell for committing this mortal sin?

I begged her to reconsider, not to have the abortion. Hannah said nothing.

A girl in our class saw Hannah leaving the doctor's office. She called out, "Hey weirdo, why did you go to see the doctor? Are you pregnant or something?" Hannah stumbled on the sidewalk, obviously distressed by what the girl had said. The girl noticed Hannah's startled response. She used this grain of truth to launch a lie so compelling that it soon swept through Kingsford. Other people embellished the story. They said Hannah was pregnant with twins. They said she had seduced a boy destined for the seminary who later committed suicide when he heard about the pregnancy. They said her mother had convinced Hannah to get pregnant so they could go after the man for child support.

Most people were surprised to hear that Hannah was pregnant. They had assumed she was a lesbian.

Brain was the first to tell me about the rumours. She whispered to me one afternoon in the library, "Some people are saying that Hannah's pregnant. If that is so, please tell her that she can come to me any time. I will help her."

Miracles

Soon Andy, our neighbours, and even Sister Agnes were asking me to confirm if the rumours of Hannah's pregnancy were correct. I feigned ignorance.

One Friday morning, the school secretary delivered a note from Father Gibson asking me to come to his office. The only students who were granted a personal audience with Father Gibson were those facing expulsion for a reprehensible act.

I showed the note to my biology teacher. She read the note, nodded and said I should leave the classroom immediately to go to Father Gibson's office. Her earnest, almost frantic, tone implied certain disaster.

My mouth was dry, my pulse trilled, as I walked down the hallway toward Father Gibson's office. I reviewed my actions in the past month, searching for a possible reason why I had been summoned. Had I said anything untoward in class that might have been cause for discipline?

Father Gibson was sitting behind his wide oak desk when I arrived at his door. He was young, not even 40, but he was a massive man, obscenely fat. He wheezed from the effort of talking.

Father Gibson made a motion for me to come in. He looked stern, gravely serious. Maybe Andy or GG has died, I thought in horror. "Shut the door and sit down." He pointed to a chair opposite him in the front of the desk.

I managed to ask timidly, "Father, is there something you needed to talk to me about?"

He looked down at papers on his desk. He did not look at me.

"It's about your friend, Hannah. There are rumours that she is with child. I need you to tell me if these rumours are true."

I assumed he could be trusted. He was, after all, a priest. I naively thought all the world was his confessional, that whatever I told him would be confidential, just between us. He asked me again if Hannah was pregnant. I told him that Hannah had been raped. I named the boy.

I cried when I told him. I said, "I am so worried about her. I don't want her to have an abortion. Someone needs to help her. Please help her."

Father Gibson was noncommittal. He told me to go back to class. He thanked me for my honesty. He made a sign of the cross in front of his face. "Blessings upon you, my child."

I returned to the classroom, plagued with an uneasy sense that things were not going to go well for Hannah.

Malignant Memory

Father Gibson called Sister Agnes to his office. He told her what I had shared with him. He visited Hannah's mother that afternoon. He told her that her daughter had sinned, that she was pregnant. Someone told the boy's family. The family lawyer later threatened to sue Hannah and her mother for defamation of character.

Hannah was suspended from school. I stopped by her house every afternoon, but her mother said that Hannah was "busy." I glimpsed her once, getting into a car. I ran after the car, but could not catch it.

Hannah and her mother left Kingsford a month later. No one knew where they had gone or if Hannah had remained pregnant.

Hannah mailed a letter for me on the day she left town. It was succinct but pointed. It simply said. "You were my friend. I trusted you with my secret. You told. Now you are no longer my friend."

I was inconsolable for a long time after Hannah left. I desperately wanted to rewrite the past, to keep Hannah's secret to myself. I vacillated between being angry at her for her desertion and disgusted at myself for my failure to keep her confidence.

During the remainder of the school year, a few nuns referred to Hannah, warning us of the evils of sin. They did not use her name. They spoke of "a girl who was once a student here." But we knew it was Hannah they were referring to. They painted Hannah as an angel who had been led astray. The true tragedy of Hannah's experience was negated by the distorted truth.

Many of my classmates who had once despised Hannah for her bullishness and crassness canonized her in her absence. They spoke of how much they missed her, what a role model she had been. I thought about how Hannah would respond to the adoration she achieved by leaving. I imagined she would tell them to all "fuck off" and that they were all "duplicitous shitheads." I smiled whenever I thought of Hannah giving them the finger from wherever she went.

I missed her vivacious presence. I missed my friend.

Hannah's leaving was a breeding ground to ready me to hear the secrets of others. It began slowly with a few confessions over several months. By the end of Grade eleven, I was hearing secrets almost daily at St. Theresa's. The caretaker, several of the students, a few teachers, and the head of the Parents Association confided their secrets to me.

Miracles

A classmate whispered to me after school was finished for the day that she had had an "unnatural longing" for one of the nuns, pretty Sister Catherine. A senior student told me in confidence in the locker room that she had stolen money from the collection plate during Mass. She told me that her father was unemployed, her family had no money. She used the stolen money to buy groceries for her family.

Secret guarding became so much part of my daily life that it never occurred to me that this was an unusual experience. I accepted that I would hear the angst of others as my lot in life. I had learned from my experience with Hannah. I told no one about the secrets others had confessed.

At home, things between Andy and GG had become peaceful, even endearing. I no longer worried about GG's welfare when I wasn't with him. Both he and Andy seemed happier.

Thelma had been right. Aphrodite helped Andy and GG to appreciate each other. Because Andy was kind and affectionate with Aphrodite, GG was no longer afraid of Andy. He began to seek her out, to enjoy her company. Because they shared a deep affection for Aphrodite, Andy began to ease off her resentment toward her father. She rarely referred to him as anything but GG. She even began to smile and laugh with him.

Andy and GG spent every available minute playing with Aphrodite. They walked her at least three times a day throughout the neighbourhood. Andy told the neighbours that Aphrodite was a "rare breed of exceptionally intelligent and loving dogs." She implied that only the truly blessed could have a dog like Aphrodite.

GG could not speak to the dog, but he managed to convey his expectations of her with touch and gestures. He taught her tricks. Aphrodite learned quickly. Soon Aphrodite was entertaining visitors by 'saying prayers', dancing on her hind legs, and burying her head in her paws as if she were ashamed. Aphrodite spent each night travelling between our beds. She curled up on the bed, providing warmth and affection to whoever was sleeping there.

Andy and GG took Aphrodite to the park when I was at school. One day, a car came perilously close to them as they walked across the street. Andy told me later, "We took a step off the curb. A car came out of nowhere. It almost ran us down. It almost killed us. I reached out to protect Aphrodite and GG. I pulled them back toward the curb. I was so relieved they were all right that I gave them both a little hug. After that, GG held my hand until we came home."

Andy was quiet for several minutes, deep in thought. She continued, "You know, it's the strangest thing. When I felt GG's little hand in mine, my heart melted. I don't really understand it, but it's changed the way I feel about him. I don't think of him as the enemy anymore. I think of him as someone who needs me."

One night, GG woke screaming. Andy and I rushed into his bedroom. He was sitting bolt upright in his bed, tears streaming down his cheeks. He was obviously terrified. Andy whispered, "A nightmare. He's had a nightmare." She sat down bedside him on the bed and gathered him into her arms. "You go back to bed," she told me. "I'll stay with him until he's feeling better."

I watched them, huddled on the bed, GG's head leaning on Andy's chest, Andy murmuring consolations to him. Miracles do happen, I thought as I returned to my bedroom.

Thelma left for her home the next day.

The furies had been exorcized.

CHAPTER TEN

BEFORE THE FALL

Grade eleven ended on a high note. I had never been more content or more confident about my future. I received awards for my academic prowess and $50 for an essay I wrote entirely in Latin about my plans for the coming summer. I missed Hannah terribly, but I had a new group of friends at school, girls like me who didn't fit in with the popular group, girls who had liked Hannah and wished they could be more like her. They were readers.

News from my family was equally gratifying. Father had drilled a third hole for a well. It had produced oil. Several oil companies courted Father. They wanted to buy the land for obscene amounts of money. Father eventually negotiated a contract with one company to purchase the farm.

Despite their relief that Paradise Lost was sold, the family did not want to move from the region. They had made friends with the neighbours. They enjoyed country living. Father astonished us all by announcing that he had come to enjoy farming. My brother Tom wrote me, "He says he loves farming. I don't know how he came to that conclusion. He left the actual farming to us boys on Paradise Lost. Now he has convinced himself that what he needed all along to love farming was money. He loves being a rich farmer."

Father and Mother purchased a lucrative farm three miles away from Paradise Lost. Photographs they sent showed their new house to be beautiful, large enough to fit their family, and sturdy. The livestock and the crops on the new farm were healthy and flourishing. Mother hired a housecleaner and a cook. Father hired help on the farm. They bought a television.

Malignant Memory

It was a relief not to worry about their livelihood any longer.

Things at home with Andy and GG were happy and peaceful. I often came home from school to see Andy and GG cuddled on the couch together, Aphrodite lying at their feet. Andy was home more often, telling the neighbours that their needs came after GG's.

The biggest news at home was that Andy had asked Crane to teach me to drive. She announced this one night after supper before the end of the school year. GG and I looked at her, startled. "It will give us more freedom to do things. We could visit Thelma. Maybe swim in her lake. We could visit your family, Ba. What do you think? We could even have a little holiday."

I had never desired to learn how to drive. I was content to be a passenger. It was no use trying to get Andy to understand this. I knew Andy well enough by then to know that once she had decided something, it was useless trying to dissuade her otherwise. It did not matter that we had no car. She would not hear my fears that I would crash into someone. I was going to learn to drive.

I practised driving Crane's car every evening. GG often accompanied us, sitting in the backseat, applauding when I accomplished another driving milestone. Crane sat beside me, gently encouraging me, telling me that I was doing fine, even when I crashed into a mailbox in my attempt to parallel park. He was extraordinarily patient. He grimaced a few times when I slammed my foot on the power brakes, nearly catapulting GG from the back seat, but he did not admonish me. "I'll never get the hang of these brakes," I would tell him. He would merely smile and say, "It takes time, Ba. Just be patient." Soon I was ready for my driver's test.

Thelma held the celebration feast at her house when I received my driver's licence. A swarm of people crowded Thelma's kitchen as her entire extended family joined us for the banquet that Thelma had prepared. Aphrodite ate samples of the meal in noisy slurps from a bowl Thelma placed on the floor.

Brain called us to attention by clinking her glass with a spoon.

"Ba was afraid to drive. She didn't think we knew that, but we did. She faced her fears and she learned to drive. She passed the driver's test with flying colours. Ba is now the family driver. She deserves a car don't you think?"

Before the Fall

Everyone applauded.

Crane took my hand and led me outside. We walked to an old garage behind Thelma's house. Crane lifted the wooden bar that closed the garage door. The garage filled with the late afternoon sunlight. I spied a car, gleaming in the sun. The car was green, although Crane assured me it was "cloud mist grey. It just looks green."

"It's a four-door, 1939 Ford Deluxe sedan," Crane told me. "I want you to have it."

"It is yours?" I asked incredulously.

"I inherited it from two women, Mrs. McLeod and Miss Chartwell. They were sisters-in-law. Mrs. McLeod was married to Miss Chartwell's brother. After Mrs. McLeod's husband died, they moved in together. They were very rich, but they had only a few friends. They were afraid that if they let people into their lives, their secret would no longer be safe. They trusted me not to tell their secret."

"Their secret?"

"Yes, their secret. The women loved each other like Brain and I love each other. They knew people would talk if they knew. I knew, but I didn't care. It's a gift to find someone else in this world that you can love so deeply.

"I used to do odd jobs for Mrs. McLeod and Miss Chartwell, things they needed done around the house. They knew I admired the car. They gave me the car as their way of saying 'thank you.'"

I was pondering this revelation when Crane began his commentary about the car. He pointed out the chrome detailing that highlighted the car's sleek appearance. He called my attention to the whitewall tires and the amber-coloured knobs and handles. He stroked the car as he talked, his pupils dilated, his voice animated.

Much of what he said was lost upon me. I had never cared about cars. I thought of them as tools to get you from one place to another. I did not need to understand its workings. His explanations of the flathead V-8 motor and hydraulic brakes seemed like gibberish.

I was amazed, though, by the condition of the car. It looked brand new. Crane explained that it had been driven only briefly by Miss Chartwell. "She was driving into town one day and she took a wrong turn. She landed up in the middle of the golf course on the twelfth green. She was so embarrassed that she never drove again." The odometer read "502."

Malignant Memory

Crane told me that that Thelma had agreed to store the car for him after he inherited it. Thelma's son, Clifford, had kept it polished and mouse-free ever since in Thelma's garage.

The car that Crane had named "Lizzie" was our source of freedom that hot and dry summer.

Andy, GG, and I went to Thelma's most days that July. We were often accompanied by Brain and Crane. We swam in the lake, laughing and splashing each other.

Brain's twisted body seemed to take on a new elegance in the water. It was as if the water obliterated her debility. She was a graceful and buoyant swimmer. A stranger would not have noticed her misshapen chest and torso, her crossed legs, when she swam.

Brain loved the water. The rest of us would be exhausted and famished, begging Brain to come out of the water so that we could rest and eat. She would agree for Crane to lift her into the chair only after our pleas became desperate. Even then, she begged Crane to put her back in the water "for just a few more minutes."

GG was an excellent swimmer, but he became cold quickly. "No padding on the man!" Andy exclaimed. "He's too thin. No wonder he shivers after a few minutes in the water." GG would mostly watch us from the shore, waving and uplifting us with silent cheers. Crane often joined him, waiting patiently for "the girls" to be ready for shore.

Once in a great while, Thelma joined us. It took painful effort for her to walk with her arthritic knees and hips from the house to the lake, but once she was in the water, her pain dissipated. She would float on her back for hours, cheerfully yelling at the turkey buzzards who circled above us in the sky, "I'm not dead yet, you miserable buzzards! Don't you be thinking you are going to taste me tonight."

In the evenings, we would watch the antics of a colony of over a hundred American white pelicans that inhabited the marshes surrounding Thelma's lake. Crane called them the "Pelican Air Force." We never tired of watching those majestic birds scooping fish into their pouches from the surface of the water and flying off in magnificent splendour into the setting sunset. The large birds waddled awkwardly on the ground like drunken sailors, but in the air, they flew like graceful ballet dancers, stunning us with their poise and elegance.

Andy and I tried on many occasions to arrange a trip to see my

Before the Fall

family on the farm that summer. Father had an exhaustive list of reasons why this was impossible. We need time to fix up the bedrooms for you. I have to go into Winnipeg for a couple of weeks to get some equipment I need. Mother has had the flu. She can't cope with visitors right now.

Andy and I admitted to each other that we were hurt by Father's diversions, but we were also concerned. "He has trouble facing up to his mistakes," Andy told me. "I am worried that somehow he's made a mess of the new farm, just like he did with the old one." I looked at her sharply. Had Andy known all along that Father had fared poorly on Paradise Lost?

Andy mused sadly, "Sometimes I wonder if all the praise everyone gave him when he was young did him any good. If it actually caused him harm. In some ways, he is still a boy. He believes all his dreams will come true if he only desires them enough."

My brother, Tom, visited us in late July. Father had paid for his ticket to Kingsford. I was surprised how tall, handsome, and articulate Tom had become. He was fun to be with, pleasant company. He complimented me on my cooking. He flattered Andy about her complexion and her housekeeping. He cheerfully played checkers with GG. Soon it seemed as if he were an integral part of our little family unit.

Tom caught us up on the family news. One of my brothers had received a prestigious scholarship to study engineering at university. Mother had a new wardrobe. She was no longer wearing overalls. The baby was thoroughly spoiled by his older siblings. Tom was in love with the neighbour's daughter. He hoped to build a house on the farm so they could live there when they were married.

Tom told us that Father had tired of the new farm and its demands shortly after moving there. "He wants to be rich. It's all he thinks about. How to get rich. He invested some of the money from the oil company in a restaurant that is going bankrupt. He purchased a factory that makes willow furniture, but there's little demand for it. He tried to raise chinchillas because he heard that there's good money in it. That was a disaster. All the chinchillas died in a couple of weeks. He is obsessed with getting money. He ignores the work that the farm needs. He ignores his family."

We were silent for several minutes. Tom's voice was sad when he continued. "The thing is, Mother is a good wife. She supports him in whatever he does. The kids are all good kids. The farm is doing well

Malignant Memory

because the boys are working hard on the farm. It will never be a rich farm, but it makes enough for all our needs. Our neighbours love us. But none of that matters to Father. He is so busy trying to get rich that he doesn't see that he is already rich."

Tom's visit was too short, only three weeks. We hugged each other tightly when he was about to board the train home. "I hated you for leaving us," he whispered into my ear. "I see now that it was good for you. You needed to escape to become the person you have become."

It was August before I knew it. Thelma's health suffered with the unrelenting August heat. Her thick, ungainly legs swelled to resemble large tree trunks. The pain in her knees and hips was severe, intractable. She could barely manage to walk a few feet without having to sit to relieve the pressure on her legs. She asked me if I could spend time at her house to help her.

I moved my belongings to Thelma's for the remainder of the summer. Andy, Brain, and Crane promised to visit me often. GG clung to me as I left.

My relationship with Thelma developed new dimensions that summer. She became my culinary guide, teaching me to cook delicacies I had only read about. She taught, sitting in a big easy chair placed near the kitchen; I did the cooking. I learned to cook moose, beaver, and pickerel cheeks. I mastered the art of making a truly fabulous bumbleberry pie. I learned how to make jam and to pickle jars of green beans, cucumbers, carrots, and beets.

I was fascinated, mesmerized, by Thelma's passion for cooking and her deep love of all food. Her food preparation rivalled the most engaging of theatre performances. She dictated how to add spices, posing in her chair as if she were a Flamenco dancer. She would sing a lively song and stamp her swollen feet on the floor to accentuate the drama of the culinary event. She often stopped to stare at what we had cooked, marvelling out loud about the attributes of the food before her. "So colourful! Like a crown of precious jewels!" She would sing a few snippets of a joyful Cree melody to mark these occasions.

In the early evening hours, Thelma and I sat in wooden deck chairs on her porch, facing her sunflower garden. Thelma loved sunflowers above all other flowers. She planted these majestic plants in a gigantic semi-circle by her front porch. Her admiration for sunflowers was a central topic of porch conversations.

Thelma would often comment that sunflowers have to have deep roots to support them as they grow to enormous heights. "We need our roots. We need to be connected to our roots in order to become who we are meant to be in life." She liked to tell me about how sunflowers bask in sunshine and only grow facing the sunlight. "We are like that, you know. We are our best when we are in the presence of love and light." She mused, "Sunflowers are such a giving flower. They give us such a wonderful display of colour in the summer, they provide seeds for the birds in the fall, and then they plant themselves again in the spring."

Thelma taught me Cree legends. She told me stories about her life. One story was about the time she went to talk to her son's teacher because he was doing badly in school. Thelma said, "She was a pretty little thing, that teacher. But she had an ugly heart. It was stained with prejudice." The teacher had assumed that Thelma was illiterate because she was Cree. The teacher told her, "You need to have someone who knows how to read and write to help your son with his homework. I understand your husband is white. Maybe he can help." Thelma had responded, "My husband is white. When I married him, he had a grade two education. I taught him how to read and write after I married him." Thelma told this story in a matter of fact way, without emotion, as if she had learned to expect racism from those who were not Cree.

One morning, I discovered a bull moose standing on Thelma's front porch as I went to get carrots from the garden. I stared at the huge animal for a few seconds. He stared back at me. I made a hasty retreat back into the kitchen.

I yelled to Thelma, "There's a big moose on the porch!" Thelma did not look up from the canning jars she was cleaning. She said calmly, "We have a message from Mr. Moose. He wants us to notice something. The moose is a symbol of endurance. Pay attention to Mr. Moose."

I opened the door. I stood on the front porch, ready to make a hasty exit. The moose ignored me. I felt uneasy being so close to such a large animal. "Give him respect," Thelma called to me.

Malignant Memory

I had no notion of how to convey respect to a moose. I simply said, "Mr. Moose, you are welcome at Thelma's house. I would appreciate it if you don't cause me harm. You are welcome to eat the flowers in the window box." The moose stared at me for a few seconds. He lumbered toward the window box at the kitchen window. He bent his head toward Thelma's petunias. Green leaves and pink petunia petals hung from the side of his mouth while he chewed his window box carnage. Soon, no flowers remained.

I backed up quietly and closed the door. I peeked out the kitchen window. The moose finally left the premises an hour later. His message went with him. We never saw him again.

Thelma's friends from the reserve often came to visit that August. Some looked unsettled when they saw me. It was clear that they had not expected that someone other than Thelma would be present. At first, I would leave the house and work in the garden until the visit was over. Soon, Thelma said, "Stay. You can listen and learn. But you must keep what our visitors say to yourself."

The visitors talked to Thelma about what had happened to them at residential school. Most said they had never revealed what happened in residential school, even to their families. Thelma said, "They try to keep what happened to them hidden. They think if they keep it buried, it won't hurt and they can forget. They don't realize that it refuses to be hidden. It will always come to life."

The visitors told about residential school hesitatingly at first, solemnly without visible emotion. They seemed to be speaking about someone else, not their self. Later, their words flowed as torrents through tears and snot. They were often unable to continue speaking until they had exhausted themselves by crying. Sometimes they became agitated, restless, walking the length of Thelma's kitchen in a frantic, tormented pace.

The visitors spoke of unimaginable horrors, of being denigrated, raped, starved, persecuted, and shamed. I tried to remain inconspicuous when the visitors were present, sitting quietly in the corner of the room. But sometimes their stories were so horrific that my gasps of shock and dismay interrupted their storytelling.

Many of the visitors spoke about how they left the residential school as young adults only to discover that they no longer felt at home in their own community when they returned. They could no longer speak their Indian language. They dressed as white people. They had little understanding of, let alone tolerance for, Indian traditions and ways. They left their home as their parents' children. They came back as strangers.

The visitors' stories of residential school were my painful education about the inhumanity of humanity. Before that summer, I believed that as I had no actual part in the abuses Thelma and others had suffered in residential school, I was blameless. The visitors' stories forced me to acknowledge my part in their history.

There was an Indian school close to Paradise Lost when I was younger. Father had pointed it out to me one day on the way to town. "That's the school for Indians," he announced. I glanced at the brick buildings with only mild curiosity. I did not question why Indian children needed a school that separated them from those who were not Indian. I don't recall ever wondering why I had never met an Indian child or why Indian children did not attend our one-room school. I did not question. And in not questioning, I became complicit in those children's abuse.

One of the most frequent of Thelma's visitors that summer was Betty, an emaciated woman in her fifties. Her face was creviced with wrinkles. She looked much older than her years. She had lost all but two of her front teeth, making her look like a wayward vampire whenever she smiled. Her fingernails were black with dirt. Her stringy grey hair was unwashed. She reeked of cheap whiskey and sometimes of urine and vomit.

Once in awhile Betty arrived at Thelma's too drunk to converse. She swayed drunkenly in Thelma's kitchen, holding up a bottle of whiskey. She shouted incoherent and unconnected words of hate to an invisible enemy. Thelma merely listened until Betty was exhausted by her tirade. She would go to Betty then, holding her in her massive arms and stroking her hair until Betty left as suddenly as she had first appeared in Thelma's kitchen.

Betty told her story of residential school in installments, a little at each visit.

In her first visits, Betty said that she had not experienced the hardships in residential school that others had spoken of. She said she was one of the lucky ones. She said that she received "treats" from the teachers at the residential school. She said she felt cared for, loved, by the staff. She assured us that her alcohol addiction "has nothing to do with residential school. That's just me being weak."

Gradually, over a number of visits, Betty revealed that the treats she had received at residential school were because she had ratted out the other children when they broke the rules. She had betrayed her friends in order to incur the staff's favour.

Betty was seven years old when she first told on another student at the school. She whispered to a teacher that her classmate, a girl she had grown up with on the reserve, had spoken Cree. Speaking Cree was strictly forbidden in the residential school. The teacher praised Betty for telling on her friend. Betty was given a chocolate for her treachery. Chocolate was a treat Betty craved. She was tired of the dull, lifeless food in the school dining room. She was hungry.

The nun strapped Betty's friend and sent her to bed without supper because of what Betty had revealed. It was the first of many occasions in which Betty gained favour from the nuns because she betrayed a friend.

Thelma listened without comment to Betty's story about her disloyalty. She held Betty lovingly on her enormous lap. Betty wailed into Thelma's gigantic bosom. She sobbed that she could not forgive herself for what she had done.

I was appalled at Betty's confession. I told myself that I would never have done what she did. I was cold and distant with Betty the next time I saw her. Thelma watched my aloofness. She said nothing.

Sometimes when we cooked together, I told Thelma about my school, the teachers, my friends. One day I told her how much I admired Sister Margaret Rose.

Thelma was stirring the jam on the stove. She looked up at me sharply. "Sister Margaret Rose you say?" I nodded. Thelma pursed her lips. Her forehead crinkled. "Ask her sometime if she ever taught at St. Francis Indian Residential School." I was confused about the anger in her voice. What was it about Sister Margaret Rose's name that angered her?

Before the Fall

I was afraid to ask Thelma how she knew Sister Margaret Rose. I did not want to know anything that tarnished my adoration of my favourite teacher. I was confident that the Sister Margaret Rose I knew had never worked at a residential school. My Sister Margaret Rose was a different one than Thelma's. My Sister Margaret Rose could never be associated with the evil that was committed in residential school.

Once Thelma asked, "Everyone has gifts, talents. What do you think are your gifts?" I was shucking corn at the time to make a chowder. The question came out of thin air. I was not expecting it. I spluttered my answer, embarrassed. "I guess I learn quickly. Well, that is, anything I am interested in. There's lots that I don't care to learn. And thanks to you, I am learning to be a better cook."

Thelma merely smiled at me. Her left eyebrow was slightly elevated, as if she were waiting for another response. She stared at me. She waited.

I was uncomfortable with the silence, with her stare. What did she want?

"Sometimes people tell me their secrets," I blurted. "I guess that's a gift. That people trust me enough to tell me their secrets. All kinds of people tell me their secrets. Kids my age, teachers, neighbours, doctors, all kinds of people. I feel like a priest, sometimes, hearing confession. But I can't give absolution for their sins."

I added after a short pause, "I never say anything when they tell me. They don't seem to need me to say anything. I just listen. And I never repeat what they tell me."

Thelma continued to watch me in silence.

"The secrets I hear—well, sometimes they are hard to hear. I have been told some things that make me afraid of what is going to happen to that person or to other people. Sometimes I can't look at the person in the same way because of what they have told me. I have even hated some people because of their secrets. Sometimes I wish people wouldn't confide in me." I was surprised to hear my own words. I had never before acknowledged aloud before that secret guarding was a painful enterprise.

Thelma merely nodded.

Later, Thelma told me a story. "When I was a little girl, we lived on the reserve. There was a bear living in the woods near the reserve. A big

Malignant Memory

black bear. He would make these terrible sounds, especially at night. He would roar and roar. He sounded fierce. He sounded mean. It scared me.

"My father became worried that the bear would attack one of the children. They had a meeting, all the men. They decided to kill the bear because the bear was a danger to the people. They killed the bear. They brought the carcass back to the reserve. The hunters were not happy. They looked sad. The bear wasn't roaring because it was mean. He had roared because there was a thorn lodged deeply in his paw. It had become infected. It was painful."

Thelma did not offer anything more about the bear and his predicament.

Much later, I told Brain about the conversation Thelma and I had about the bear who roared. I told Brain smugly, "I know what it means. It means that I shouldn't judge the people who tell me secrets because I don't know if they have a thorn in their paw. I can't know what caused them to do the things they did, or to be who they are."

Brain smiled up at me. "Be careful that you don't interpret Thelma's stories too quickly. They usually have meanings that are deep within the story. You discover those meanings after you chew on the story for a long time."

I was convinced that my interpretation of the story was the correct one. I vowed to simply accept the secrets that were given to me to guard. I would not judge secret tellers.

I did not know then that the true and devastating meaning of Thelma's story would be revealed in the time to come.

CHAPTER ELEVEN

PORTENT

I was so content living with Thelma that I overlooked the inevitability of summer's passing. I was caught off guard when fall arrived without warning. The mornings were cool; the leaves on the trees changed colours. Thelma's sunflowers drooped their heads in defeat. I shrugged off the unhurried, reflective moments of summer and made room for the busyness of my final year at high school.

I was eager to start school. My friends were happy to see me. We shared summer memories in frantic whirrs of conversation. Foremost on our minds was what each of us planned to do after graduation. I pronounced with a certainty known only to those who know no better that I was going to be a famous author. It seemed to me on that first day of school that everything I dreamed of was an easy reach, that every dream I had was mine for the taking.

It was a delightful surprise to learn that Sister Margaret Rose was now teaching history. A rumour circulated throughout St. Theresa's that literature had been removed from Sister Margaret Rose's teaching assignment because she had included books that were not in the assigned curriculum. The assumption was that she could not stray from the history curriculum because history is factual.

History taught by Sister Margaret Rose was a joyful and provocative experience. It was in Sister Margaret Rose's history class that I learned to question what was written in our school texts about our history. It was Sister Margaret Rose who taught me that there are multiple ways of viewing the same events; that the "facts" are often merely subjective accounts born out of personal agendas.

Malignant Memory

Sister Margaret Rose gave us an assignment to be completed by the end of the school year. We were to write a 20-page essay in response to a quote by Ralph Waldo Emerson, "All history becomes subjective; in other words, there is properly no history, only biography." I knew immediately what I would write about—residential schools. It was my attempt to make sense of why I, and most others in Kingsford, had never heard about residential schools and knew little about the crimes that had been committed there.

Brain was invaluable in helping me to locate facts about residential schools. "Very few people apart from those who went there know what really went on in residential schools. You'll want to back up the people's stories with documented evidence," she cautioned. "Otherwise, your teacher will find it hard to believe that the stories are true."

Documented evidence was almost impossible to locate in the 1960s. It was Brain who located a speech made by Canada's first Prime Minister, Sir John A. MacDonald, on the subject of residential schools. He had declared that residential schools were necessary to inject white man's culture into the "savages" that were Indian children. I thought about the gentle, kind Cree people who had embraced Andy, GG, and I when we visited Thelma. I felt sick to my stomach at his words.

Brain found some archived photographs of children sitting in residential school classrooms. The children in the photograph stared up at the photographer listless and sad. Not one of the children was smiling.

Brain also located reviews of residential schools that warned that the conditions in residential schools were abhorrent, placing the children's health at great risk. The authors indicated that many of the children had died while in residential school. The details of the children's deaths were often vague. The earliest of these documents was dated 1907. The latest was the previous year. The author of the most current review stated that prior reviews had produced no concerted efforts to improve the conditions in residential schools; the situation remained as dire as it had ever been.

Thelma was eager to help me with my essay. We sat in her kitchen for many hours as she told story after story about her experiences in residential school. She took me to meet her best friend, Bert. They had lived next door to each other when they were young. They went to the same residential school. Thelma told me, "He went to the boys' section.

Portent

I went to the girls'. We never saw each other. We didn't talk to each other until we were teenagers, out of school and back home."

Bert was a cheerful, quiet man with a broad smile. He agreed to tell me what he had experienced. "It wasn't all bad," he told me. "Well, most of it was bad, but there were some good moments. One of the priests gave me my first pair of ice skates."

Thelma talked to her friends about my project. She asked them to share their experiences of residential school with me. Many were sceptical. "Why would a white girl want to know about those things?" Some told Thelma they could not bear to talk about their experiences to anyone. Thelma promised her friends that they could decide what went in the essay. I would not disclose anything that they did not want me to share with others. "I told them you guard secrets," Thelma said. "I told them that you are trustworthy." Five people said they would tell me their story. They had attended the same residential school but at different times.

Carl told of being seven years old and being chased by a priest into the woods surrounding the school. The priest finally caught up to Carl. He raped him. The priest raped him many times over the years. He raped him until the boy became old enough to fight off the priest's advances.

What was striking was that Carl forgave the rapist priest. Carl remained a practising Catholic.

"How can you still be a Catholic when a priest did that to you?" I asked him.

"There are bad apples in every bushel," he answered. "I love the Church. It wasn't the Catholic Church who raped me."

Myrtle told me, "I never knew a loving parent at residential school. Our 'parents' were the nuns and the priests. They were strict. They almost never smiled. They didn't cuddle us or play games with us. They hit us when we didn't obey their rules. They told us our real parents were ignorant savages. They said we shouldn't do anything our real parents did. Only the white man's ways were good. I shut down emotionally. I developed a hard shell around my feelings. So when I became a parent, I was terrible at it. I had no models of what a good parent was. My kids suffered for it. Now my grandchildren are suffering because their parents had no good model for being a parent."

Malignant Memory

Over time, I became more and more aware of the profound privilege I was being granted to hear the stories. I was humbled by the storytellers' grace and compassion in the light of the terrible wrongs that had been perpetrated on them.

Thelma asked me one day when I was visiting her if I had noticed that Crane was unusually pale. Crane had visited her that afternoon. Thelma said she was worried about him. "He seems tired. I watch him walk and he is in pain."

I was startled by Thelma's observations. I hadn't allowed myself to take note of the changes in Crane. She was right that he was less energetic. He winced sometimes when he thought we weren't watching. It was too confusing, too dreadful, to imagine that Crane might not be the virile and steadfast support he had always been to us. I told Thelma I had not noticed these things. I lied. It was an escape from the anxiety Thelma's words had interjected in my world.

I was in the library one day when Crane asked me if I could take Brain up to the second floor washroom. I was startled, looking up at him in a puzzled way. "You've never asked me to do this before," I told him. "Are you okay?"

"I'm fine." Crane looked down at the book he was reading, avoiding my eyes. "I just want to read my book."

I was not convinced. He seemed tired. His complexion was pasty.

"What's happening with Crane? He's not himself lately," I said to Brain in the washroom. She was busy fiddling with her catheter bag, draining the urine into the toilet. She hesitated before she responded. "He's not been sleeping well lately. His back has been bothering him." She looked up at me sharply. "He won't go to the doctor about it." She added angrily, "What can I do if he won't get help? He's so stubborn!"

I watched Crane more closely after that. He often fell asleep on his book at the library table. He let out an involuntary groan when he lifted Brain in her wheelchair. He never acknowledged to us that he was in pain or uncomfortable in any way. He answered curtly, "Fine" whenever I inquired how he was. He said it in such a way as to convey that the conversation had ended.

I developed a dictionary of Crane's pain. Holding his palm to the lower back was an indication of severe pain. Hesitating before he climbed the stairs to the second floor of the library meant that he was

Portent

in moderate pain, but afraid that the effort would exacerbate the pain to intolerable levels. Being unusually abrupt when Brain asked him to carry her up the stairs was a sign that he had had enough. He could no longer tolerate the discomfort.

Gradually, I took over Crane's role as Brain's assistant whenever I was in the library. Brain thanked me for helping her. "You are so good to do this for us, Ba. Unfortunately, there is no one to help us when you are at school. I try not to ask Crane for anything, but sometimes it can't be helped."

Andy brought GG to the library one afternoon. She said to me later that evening, "I was shocked when I saw Crane today. He's lost a lot of weight. And he's as pale as snow. I am worried about him."

The thought that Crane was ill niggled at the back of my brain, but the essay about residential schools eclipsed any other thoughts. I was totally immersed in it.

One afternoon I went to the library. Andy was there, GG too. Andy was running up and down the stairs, doing errands for Brain. Brain said, "She's here every day when I get to the library in the morning. She and GG get things for me all day. Andy brings a lunch for us. She takes me to the washroom when I need to go. She usually goes home before you get here, but today she was caught up doing something on the third floor." Brain paused. She said softly, sadly, "Andy and GG have helped me so much. Crane just can't do what he used to do."

I looked over at Andy, overwhelmed by her selfless compassion. She had not mentioned a word of what she had been doing to help Brain. I walked to where she was standing on the stairs. I put my arms around her waist and hugged her. "I love you," I told her.

Andy patted my hair awkwardly. "That's enough, now," she said, embarrassed. "We have work to do."

Andy told me later that evening that Crane had finally gone to the doctor. "He has cancer of the spine. It's travelled to other parts of his body too. He is very sick. The doctor said he will probably die in a few months."

GG and I sat silently while the enormity of Andy's words settled in us.

Andy spoke what I was thinking. "I don't know how Brain will manage without him. She depends on him for everything."

Malignant Memory

Andy and I cried together on the couch for the loss of Crane that we had not yet experienced and could barely believe. GG sat at our feet, resting his head in Andy's lap. Aphrodite lay beside him.

Andy telephoned Thelma later that evening. It was a tearful conversation between two good friends. I overheard Andy say, "How will we all manage without him? Our strong quiet hero? Our Crane?" I went to bed that night older in my spirit, angry that wonderful people like Brain and Crane had to suffer the indignities of cancer, and overcome with sadness for the loss we would experience at Crane's death.

Crane became visibly weaker in the following weeks. It was as if the diagnosis had stripped him of pretense. He no longer tried to do the things he had done when he was officially well. He allowed himself some relief of the pain by taking narcotics prescribed to him by the physician. He retired to a bed placed in the living room of their house. He devoted himself to the work of dying.

Brain and Crane were well loved in Kingsford. People wanted Crane to know how much he meant to them. There were numerous visitors the first month of Crane's confinement. The little house was crowded with caregivers, well-meaning visitors, and curious spectators. Brain and Crane's dogs added to the frenzied activity in the house by yapping in a frantic chorus every time someone entered the house. The cats hid under the furniture.

Andy said irritably after a visit to Brain and Crane's house, "You practically have to trip over people just to say hello to Crane. Most of them are so focussed on saying good-bye to Crane that they don't notice how tired he is. They don't see his pain."

The visitors brought mountains of food. Brain accepted their edible offerings with gratitude, but she told me privately, "Neither Crane or I have an appetite. We have no room left in our fridge. I throw out most of what they bring. I appreciate their kindness though."

Brain was confident that she could address the chaos in their house. "Our house isn't even ours anymore," she said. "We need some alone time together. I will figure out what to do to."

The first thing she did was to tell all the visitors kindly but firmly. "It is very important that Crane gets his rest right now. I am sure you want what's best for him. He is very grateful for the love and support you have given him. But now he needs to rest." She suggested to those

Portent

who argued that they needed to say something personally to Crane that they write letters instead. She asked Crane's best friend, Jim, the local undertaker, to be the family "reporter." "I want you to be the person that tells all the others what's happening, all the news. Make it clear that they are not to be phoning us or coming by unless I have told you that it's okay. You are the official traffic controller in this house from now on!" Jim agreed to assume this role.

Thanks to Brain's interventions, Brain and Crane reclaimed their house as theirs once again.

The pets were gone from the house by the end of November. A pyramid of pet toys lay in the corner of the living room as a monument to the animals Brain and Crane had loved. "We can't manage them anymore," Brain told me. "I found good homes for all of them. They will be fine. Crane is my focus now." Brain seemed resolute, almost unfeeling about the loss of her beloved pets. I could not imagine that she wasn't experiencing these losses deeply.

A few friends offered to take Brain to and from the library. Some offered to stay with her throughout her shifts to help her in whatever way they could. These were well-meaning offers, but they were not without issue. Some people who had promised to be at the library to help Brain later reneged because of other commitments or simply did not show up when they had promised to be there. A few were vocal about how demanding it was to assist Brain in the library.

"My independence is very important to me," Brain told me. "I have fought to be independent all my life. When I have to ask people for things, or when I am late because of someone else I feel dependent and helpless. I hate that! I have decided to retire by the end of June. I will be with Crane. He needs me."

Andy and GG continued to go to the library to assist Brain every day. GG was showing the strain. One afternoon, we discovered GG asleep in the library stacks, curled in a ball on the wood floor. Andy whispered to me, "I don't know how much longer I can ask him to do this. I know he wants to help, but he's getting very tired."

Brain was also showing signs of the strain. Her clothes were often dishevelled. Her hair was greasy and unwashed. She often lost her train of thought, stopping mid-sentence to remember what she was doing or saying. She rarely smiled and even then, her smile was forced. She

Malignant Memory

was unusually curt with customers. Her conversations with them were restricted to library business. She no longer entertained chats or inquired about their well-being. Complaints began to filter in to the municipal office about Brain's performance as a librarian.

Andy and I discussed how to address the changes in Brain, particularly her deteriorating comportment. We knew that Crane was no longer able to help her with her bathing and dress. Brain was not able to manage this on her own. We agreed that it would be very touchy to talk to Brain about this. She was fiercely independent. She would not appreciate being reminded that she was not able to care for herself.

Andy sent me to retrieve Thelma. "Thelma will know how to talk to Brain."

I drove Thelma to Brain and Crane's house. When Thelma told Brain that she was staying with them for a week, Brain cried with relief. She reached out her arms to receive Thelma's embrace. Crane smiled at them both from his bed.

Thelma's presence at Brain and Crane's house was a gift of peace. I don't know what Thelma said or how she said it, but she managed to help Brain see that she needed assistance with her grooming. Brain sent me a note via Thelma. The note read, "Dear Ba, You are so dear to Crane and me. We trust you with everything. I have hired someone to do the laundry, but I need your help to wash me. I need you to give me a bath every couple of days. I know this is an imposition because you are so busy right now as you finish school, but I would really appreciate it. Could you do this thing for me please?"

"Tell her, yes!" I told Thelma. "Tell her I will be glad to do it."

Andy and I prepared for the Christmas season in an exhausting frenzy, as if our futures and that of our friends depended on the exquisiteness of decorations, baking, and gifts. We were determined that the good will of Christmas would surpass the recent tragedy of Crane's illness that had shattered our hopes and bruised our souls.

Just as Christmas cards and advertisements promised, wondrous things happened that season. Both Brain and GG regained some of their verve with a break from the library. Brain looked much like her former self. She was clean, well-dressed, and she smelled only of the soap I used in her baths.

Portent

I prepared a feast on Christmas Day at Brain and Crane's house. Thelma and some of her family joined us. Aphrodite did her utmost to fill the void that the missing pets had left. Crane slept most of the evening, waking only to smile at us or to receive Brain's kisses. The rest of us ate, laughed, and wore silly hats from our Christmas crackers.

Despite our efforts, the sadness that permeated the little house was inescapable. Andy said later that she thought we had "forced Christmas on ourselves, trying to make out like there wasn't a dying man in the room."

CHAPTER TWELVE

DECISIONS

I returned to school after the Christmas break, excited to hand in my essay about residential schools to Sister Margaret Rose. I felt it was the best essay I had ever written. I knew Sister Margaret Rose would be moved by the power of the stories. I imagined how I would respond when she rewarded me with the highest grade for the essay. I saw myself showing the A+ and Sister Margaret Rose's complimentary comments to the storytellers. I visualized their delight in knowing that their stories had elicited such attention and praise.

Thelma invited all the storytellers to come to her house for the final reading of the essay before I submitted it to Sister Margaret Rose. Everyone was quiet for a long time when I finished speaking. Bert was the first to comment. "It makes me glad to know that someone who doesn't know about this part of our history will understand a little more about what residential schools did to our people." Myrtle hugged me. "Even if no one reads this but your teacher, I am glad that you listened to our stories. I am happy that you want to understand."

Some of the storytellers told me much later that they had been plagued with sadness for weeks after they told me of the pain they experienced in residential school. Josie confided that she felt "all out of sorts since I have been reliving these stories with you." Thelma said, "Telling the stories to you was good, but I can feel the furies trying to gain a foothold again."

Two weeks after I submitted the essay, Sister Margaret Rose asked to speak privately to me after class. I was confident that she was about to heap praises upon me. I sat down opposite her at her desk. She was flushed.

Malignant Memory

She looked at me for several seconds as if searching my face for an answer to an unknown question.

"The residential school you talk about. That's St. Francis, isn't it?"

I nodded.

"The Thelma in your essay, was that Thelma Piche by any chance?"

"Her name is Thelma Hardy now. Piche was her name before she got married."

"I knew her. I knew your Thelma. At the residential school."

I gasped. I felt frantic, afraid. I prayed silently, "Please don't tell me you did cruel things to Thelma or the others."

Sister Margaret Rose bent her head. I could not see her eyes. She folded her hands in her lap as if in supplication. She spoke slowly, her voice barely above a whisper.

"I was eighteen when I went into the convent. I had wanted to be a nun most of my life. I was filled with good intentions. I thought I'd be a positive force in the world, that I'd do God's work and make the world a better place. I was naïve.

"I was in the convent for two years as a noviciate. It was quite good really. I thought I had found my true calling in life. I was happy.

"After I took my final vows, Mother Superior told me they were sending me for training to become a teacher. I had never thought of myself as a teacher. I wanted to be a nurse. But I had taken the vow of obedience, so I went to become a teacher.

"It was a surprise to me when I discovered I loved being a teacher. I loved making the children laugh, to have fun, while they were learning. But then they sent me to be a teacher at St. Francis, a residential school for Indian children.

"At first, it was a wonderful experience. They were lovely children. So far away from home, so eager for love. The little ones would climb up into my lap for a cuddle. I would kiss and hug them. I taught them songs and little dances. They taught me Cree words. They told me about their families.

"But then I was disciplined.

"Mother Superior called me into her office. She handed me a list of rules. I was not allowed to show any affection to a child. I could not touch them except to strap them. I could not tell them they were special. I was not to laugh with the children. The only music I could teach was hymns. Dancing was not allowed. Mother Superior assigned

Decisions

me the tasks of scrubbing floors and laundering the children's bed sheets as punishment for the infractions I had already committed."

Sister Margaret Rose lifted her head slowly. I saw tears in her eyes. She turned away from me to stare out the window, unseeing.

"I had to obey her, you see. I had taken the vow of obedience. I did what she asked of me. But I had to cultivate a coldness around my heart in order to do what she commanded me to do. A part of me died when I obeyed her rules. I lost who I was. I became someone I did not like. I felt no joy anymore. I did not enjoy the children. Instead I found fault with them. I went through the rituals of prayer but felt nothing. My deep love of God was gone.

"One evening, I came across Thelma and Eva. They were friends. They were about the same age, twelve or so. They had come from the same reserve. They were hiding in a closet.

"I listened behind the door for awhile. I heard them whispering about a plan to have Eva escape from the school and go back home. They looked terrified when I opened the door. I demanded to know what they were doing. Eva clung to Thelma. She had been crying. Her eyes were red, her cheeks stained with tears. She looked miserable, poor child.

"Eva was a skinny little girl. You could count her ribs through her shirt. She had TB before she came to St. Francis. She was sickly. I didn't really know her before I met her in the closet. She almost never talked. She was one of those children that look like they want to disappear.

"Thelma was usually timid and quiet, but now she stood up and faced me directly. She was short—she only came up to my stomach—but she looked fierce. She told me in no uncertain terms, in a booming voice, that I had to help Eva.

"Thelma could have been in a lot of trouble for planning Eva's escape, for speaking to me in such an impertinent way. Students had been beaten, starved, for lesser offences.

"I was so unnerved by Thelma's courage, by her confidence, that I listened. Thelma told me that Eva's mother was gravely ill. Her mother was expected to die within the week. Eva asked Mother Superior if she could go to her mother before her mother died. Mother Superior refused. Mother Superior gave no rationale for this decision. She simply said, "No. Get back to class."

Malignant Memory

"Mother Superior had told us about Eva's request at supper, before I found the girls hiding in the closet. She said that Eva was known to be a runaway. Eva had tried to escape from the school several times before. Mother Superior told us to keep a close watch on Eva. "She's going to run. She will want to be with her mother. Don't let her out of your sight."

"I don't remember having any particular reaction to Mother Superior's announcement. It was just the way she was with the children. She treated them as if every one of them was bad at their core.

"It was when I couldn't find Eva at bedtime that I went looking for her.

"Thelma told me that if I had any heart at all, I would help sneak Eva out of the school so she could return to her home to be with her mother. I don't know why Thelma asked me. I had never been very kind to her.

"I felt the stirrings of compassion as Thelma pleaded with me. It had been a long time since I had experienced care for a child in the school. I felt my shrivelled heart stretch with empathy for Eva and for the sadness of her situation. I began to think that Mother Superior was unnaturally cruel not to allow Eva to go home. I began to be angry.

"I knew I had to help Eva get home.

"So Thelma and I launched a plan to sneak Eva out of the school. We knew we needed to distract the other nuns from watching Eva. Eva would need supplies. Eva's home was three hours away by foot. It was winter. It was very cold that night.

"Thelma created a distraction in the dining room at lunch time. She started screaming hysterically, throwing cutlery, and lurching like she was having a seizure. The other nuns rushed to her, yelling at her to keep quiet. One of them strapped her around her face and neck. Later, Thelma was severely punished for making such a commotion.

"When all the others were looking at Thelma, I hurried Eva out of the dining room. I had stolen some food from the kitchen. I found some warm clothes and boots in a bin of dead children's clothes. I took Eva to the nun's quarters and let her out the door at the back. Eva looked so scared, so wretched, that I hugged her. I told her I would pray for her safe journey. I would pray for her mother. Eva simply nodded.

Decisions

"After Eva left, I got down on my knees and I prayed. I prayed with every fibre of my being. For the first time in a very long time, I felt God at the other end of my prayers.

"The other nuns found Eva was missing about an hour later. They sent the caretaker and his dogs after her. The caretaker found Eva and brought her back to the school. She was locked in a room. They strapped her over and over. Eva never told them how she escaped. She said she had stolen the food and clothes herself.

"One week later, Eva's mother died. Mother Superior asked that I bring Eva to the office to hear the news. I found Eva hanging in a closet. Her face was blue, her jaw slack. But she looked peaceful, as if she had finally found her way home."

Sister Margaret Rose turned to face me, tears streaming down her cheeks.

"I was ill after Eva died. Ill for a long time. I heard voices. I saw things that were not there. I had to go to a hospital. I was there until the summer before I came to St. Theresa's.

"It has been healing to teach once more. In teaching all you precious young people, I found my joy again. But I am deeply ashamed of some of the things I did at St. Francis. I am haunted by the cruel things I did to those dear children. I am finding it hard to forgive myself."

I listened, relieved to hear that Sister Margaret Rose felt remorse for what she had done, but at the same time, incensed that she had contributed to the degradation that Thelma and my Cree friends had related to me. The admiration and hero worship I once felt for Sister Margaret Rose was now tainted.

Sister Margaret Rose handed me my essay. It had not been graded. She explained why.

"The essay deserves an A+. It is exceptional. What you have written I know is true. I witnessed and participated in some of the same travesties that you describe in your essay.

"But if I give you an A+, Sister Agnes will want to read it. She reads all essays that receive a grade of A+. It's her policy.

"And I need you to know that Sister Agnes will be very angry. I have heard her talk about people who say that cruelty happened in residential schools. She thinks it's all lies. She will not want to read

Malignant Memory

that our beloved Church had any part in victimizing these children. She will accuse you of making all this up, of trying to get attention by sensationalizing what the Church did to help Indian children. And she has the final word in grades so you'll probably receive an F."

Sister Margaret Rose paused. When she continued, her tone was strident, imploring.

"It's up to you. Your marks in high school have all been As and A+s. You are in line for some of the biggest scholarships given by the school. An F would mean that you probably would not be considered as a candidate for a scholarship.

"I know you need a scholarship to afford university. It would be a shame if you couldn't go to university because of an F."

She paused. When she began again, she was gentle, pleading. "On the other hand, I could give you a B+, and Sister Agnes would never have to read your essay. A B+ would probably be overlooked by the scholarship committee in light of all your other marks."

Sister Margaret Rose bent her head toward me, as if sharing a secret. She whispered, "If Sister Agnes knew I had given you an A+, she would be furious with me. She would discipline me. I might lose the history class. She would punish me by giving me something like mathematics or geography. I would be miserable. I couldn't bear it."

Her final words to me were, "It's your choice. You let me know whether you want me to give you the A+ you deserve and risk Sister Agnes' wrath, or whether you want me to give your essay a B+ and the contents of the essay will not be shared with anyone but you and me."

I stumbled out of the classroom, too confused to articulate my thoughts or feelings.

I stopped at the library before I went home. I spied Brain at her desk. I burst into tears. She led me to a back room. I sobbed until no tears were left. Brain listened without interruption as I poured out the details of what had happened about the essay. I did not tell her about Sister Margaret Rose's confession, only the decision I had to make about the grade on the essay.

Brain took the essay from me and quickly scanned Sister Margaret Rose's notes in the margins.

"It is one of the hardest things in life to discover that your heroes are not perfect," she said. "Sister Margaret Rose is cowardly not to take

Decisions

a stand against Sister Agnes on your behalf. But she has taken a vow of obedience and she has to do what Sister Agnes tells her.

"I have read your essay. It is brilliant. You wrote so well. It was a passionate essay about an important subject. But when people feel threatened, they lash out. Sister Margaret Rose is telling you that Sister Agnes will feel threatened about what you wrote—not because it isn't true, but because it is. If Sister Agnes admits what you wrote is true, it calls into question everything she believes about Indians, about the Church, about herself. If you want to win a scholarship and go to university, you might just have to settle for a lesser grade than an A+."

Brain told Crane what I had divulged. His response was unusually direct. "There's no way you should take less than an A+ for your essay. Not just because your writing deserves that grade, but because to take less than an A+ dishonours the people who shared their stories with you. If you compromise your grade on this essay, it will imply that the stories people shared with you are not credible or important. You have to take a stand, even if it costs you a scholarship."

Andy was pensive when I told her what had happened. She surprised me by agreeing with Crane. She sat on the couch with me, holding my hand. "We will find a way for you to go to university, even if you don't get a scholarship. A scholarship is nice, but it isn't worth compromising your integrity."

I visited Thelma the next day. I told her that Sister Margaret Rose was the same nun she remembered. I did not tell her what Sister Margaret Rose had told me about her.

Thelma peered in my eyes. "I see you know about Eva," she said. When I told Thelma about Sister Margaret Rose's suggestion that I decide the fate of the essay, her reaction was composed. "I guess you will have to decide," she said calmly.

"Aren't you angry that Sister Agnes could dismiss the stories in the essay?" I asked incredulously.

Thelma reached out to touch my cheek gently. "Honey, if I got angry every time I met a bigot or someone who refused to see the bad that has been done to my people, I would have exploded by now. My anger hurts me more than it affects them. They are so convinced they are right that my anger just confirms what they already believe—that we are savages."

Malignant Memory

Thelma suggested I meet with those who had shared their stories for the essay and tell them what had transpired. The storytellers listened patiently to what Sister Margaret Rose had proposed. They were divided about what I should do. Myrtle and Carl thought that I should settle for a B+. "That way you'll be able to go to university, and then someday you will work with us to make the stories of residential school be heard across the country."

Bert believed strongly that I should be prepared to risk Sister Agnes' retribution. Josie agreed with him.

Bert said, "That teacher of yours, that Sister Margaret Rose, she was wrong to make the decision yours. She's the teacher. It's her job to give the grade. Telling you to decide is her way of distancing herself from what you wrote. If she gives you a B+, then the essay stays between the two of you. If she gives you an A+, then Sister Agnes may choose to say it's all a fabrication. Either way, our stories will never be shared."

Betty was the only one who did not tell me what I should do. She simply said, "Trust your heart. Do what you think is right."

I slept fitfully that week, unable to decide the best course of action. In the end, I decided to accept the B+. I needed a scholarship. Andy had promised that she would find a way to fund my education, but she had few resources to do so. My parents were rapidly devouring the monies from the oil company, and they would not be able to contribute. I imagined my graduation day, and I cringed when I pictured my name as missing among the list of scholarship winners. I visualized my parents' embarrassment, my own humiliation. I rationalized that winning a scholarship would be the ticket to become someone with a university education who would have the credibility and power to defeat the bigotry that Thelma and her friends encountered.

Thelma and Sister Margaret Rose met one afternoon in February. Crane drove Thelma to St. Theresa's so that they could talk together. I do not know who initiated the visit. I do not know what they talked about. Thelma would only say that the meeting had been a good one. "We offered healing to one another through our tears." Sister Margaret Rose never mentioned the visit to me.

I was distant with Sister Margaret Rose after the experience with the essay. She tried initially to talk to me about what I was feeling and thinking about the decision about the essay, but I rebuffed her attempts.

Decisions

My feelings about Sister Margaret Rose were complicated, a mixture of love and hate, forgiveness and unforgiveness. I was sad for what she had experienced in the residential school. I was concerned about the vulnerability of her mental health. I was grateful for how good a teacher she had been to me. But I could not forget that she was not courageous enough to present the essay as it was to Sister Agnes.

The distancing was protective. I could not bear the possibility that she might disappoint me more than she had already done.

Sister Margaret Rose left the convent the day before our convocation. No one in the school had known her intention to leave. I learned later that she had asked to say good-bye to her students, but was not permitted to do so. The grief of the students when they heard the news was palpable. Thelma's response when I told her about Sister Margaret Rose's leaving was typically perplexing. "Sometimes the only way we find out that a hole is too tight for us is to get stuck in the hole."

In the end, I did win a scholarship, the largest in the school. It would enable me to attend the university of my choice for four years, with all expenses paid. Sister Agnes made the announcement at my graduation. She spoke of how I was lacking a basic foundation for higher education when I had arrived from the farm, that I had no religious upbringing. She raved about my prowess, my potential. She implied that it had been her guidance, her direction, that had whipped me into shape to become a scholarship winner.

I looked into the audience. I saw Thelma, Brain, GG, and Andy beaming at me in pride. I saw Crane, his head bent, asleep in his chair. He was gaunt, emaciated. His pallor was striking. I had a lump in my throat when I thought about how much the effort of attending my graduation had cost him.

I did not feel any of the celebratory joy that day.

CHAPTER THIRTEEN

REVELATIONS

By the end of June, Crane was so weak that he could no longer walk on his own to the bathroom. He was frail. His arms and legs were pencil-thin. His formerly impressive muscles lay deflated on his bones. Circles under his eyes grew darker and deeper each day.

Brain retired from the library. She reluctantly attended the retirement party offered to her by the municipal office. More than 300 people came to wish her well and thank her. They brought gifts, letters explaining what she had meant to them, and overdue books they had been meaning to return. Some gave impromptu speeches.

One speech maker was a university professor. He had travelled from England to be there. The man told how Brain had spent time with him every day after the library closed to teach him how to read. Before that, he had been unable to read in school. The man said, "She believed in me when everyone else had given up hope. I try to follow her example whenever I am with a student who struggles. I can only aspire to be as loving and as skilled as Brain is in helping young people to love reading."

Brain seemed very far away, as if none of the words could penetrate her consciousness. I tried to reach her by pointing out that the day had demonstrated how much people cared about her, how special she was. Brain simply looked at me sadly and said, "I just want this to be over. I want to be home with Crane."

Brain became quieter and more fiercely determined over the next weeks. She rarely smiled and when she did, it was forced. Despite her physical limitations, Brain found ways to climb onto Crane's bed to wash him, feed him, and change his pajamas. She alone administered his medications. Brain became Crane's sole caregiver.

Brain zealously guarded her time with Crane. "I want every moment I can with him," she declared to Andy and I. She refused to permit the nurses to provide Crane's daily care. She told the doctor that he could visit only at her command. "I will let you know if we need you. Otherwise, we don't want you to visit."

I was hurt when Brain made it clear that she did not want me to visit any longer. She did not try to sugarcoat the message. She made it very clear that she was in charge. She delivered the message with a harshness that was unfamiliar to me. "I want to be alone with Crane for the little time we have left," she told me. "I have hired a nurse to give me my bath. You don't need to do that anymore. I will let you know if I want you to come over."

Andy tried to soothe my bruised ego. "Brain won't let Thelma, GG, or I visit either. Try not to take it personally. Thelma says that Brain is just trying to hold onto Crane and their life together. Her heart is broken. Let's just keep trying to let her know that we are there for her, for both of them. She'll let us know when we can help."

Brain telephoned me the next week. There were no pleasantries, no small talk. She said, "Crane has an idea that he would like to write letters to some people before he dies. He wants to dictate them to you. Could you come over tomorrow for the afternoon so he can dictate the letters to you?"

I knocked on the front door of the little house the next day. Brain let me into the living room. All the curtains had been drawn. No lights were on. The house was in darkness. I could barely make out Crane sitting on the edge of his bed.

"I am going out to do some errands," Brain announced. "The paper and everything you need is beside Crane's bed. Jim is taking me to do errands. I will be back in an hour." She did not look at me when she spoke.

Her abruptness stung. I forced myself to remember Andy's words. I smiled at Brain. "We'll be fine," I told her. I was friendly, cheerful. Brain kissed Crane full on the lips. She lingered over him, memorizing his face. She left the house without saying anything further.

Crane asked me to come to his bedside for a hug. He was not a demonstrative man to anyone but Brain. I had never been hugged by

Revelations

him before. I angled my body over the bed in an awkward pose, waiting for his embrace. I was surprised how good his hug felt. "I have missed you, Ba," he said.

Crane lay back on the bed and grimaced with pain. "I don't know how much we will get done today," he told me. "I just took some of my pain medication. I may doze off. Let's see what we can do." He paused. He was serious, pointed, when he spoke again. "I know you keep secrets. These letters are secret between me and the person I am writing to. Even Brain won't know what I have written. You won't reveal anything I wrote in the letters, promise?"

I nodded in assent.

Crane asked me to open the curtains. "It's so dark in here," he said. "Brain likes it dark. I find it depressing."

I sat at a chair by the head of the bed while Crane dictated the first letter. It was to Mrs. Dixon, the woman who ran the corner grocery store. I did not know that they were friends.

Crane spoke. I wrote. The dictation was slow. At times, Crane struggled for the right words. His voice became weaker and harder to hear as the dictation went on. Twice, he fell asleep in the middle of a sentence and did not waken for several minutes. Once he said he needed to rest because the pain was too severe. Another time, he asked me to help move him because he was uncomfortable lying on his back. He let out a scream when I pushed him onto his side. It took time before he was settled enough to continue the dictation.

Crane's letter to Mrs. Dixon read:

"My Dear Mrs. Dixon,

As you probably know, I have cancer. I am expected to die within the month. I have been lying in my bed lately with nothing to do but think. I have been remembering the numerous times I have come into your store. I can see your lovely smile. You would always ask about me and Brain. You never forgot our dogs' names. You always apologized when you didn't have something I had come for. But the next time I went to your store, you would remember and tell me that you had the item now. I know that sometimes you had to order the item especially for us.

Mrs. Dixon, I have known you for over 40 years, but still I barely know you. We never talked about your life at all. I could see for myself how long the hours were that you worked and how clean you

Malignant Memory

kept the store. But I never knew if you had children or what happened to Mr. Dixon. I never asked you how you got into the grocery business in the first place. I have no idea about your goals or what you think of living in Kingsford.

It is a peculiar thing that I know little about you and yet, you are one of the people I wanted to be sure to say good-bye to. I think it's because you always looked pleased to see me, even when you must have been exhausted by the day's work. I do not flatter myself that this response was reserved for me alone. I have watched you with other customers and you are the same with them.

So, Mrs. Dixon, I would like to say good-bye and thank you. You have made my life a more pleasant experience by being who you are. I have appreciated the way you made the simple act of buying a few groceries something that I looked forward to. There is so much in life that is cruel and harsh. Your kindness and your goodness have made my world a better place.

With fond memories
Crane"

Crane told me to place the letter in an envelope. He asked me to address it to Mrs. Dixon. "Take the letter with you and put it in a safe place in your house. After I'm gone, please deliver all the letters for me. There are lots of letters still to dictate. Do you think you could come again tomorrow?" I nodded.

Brain returned promptly at the hour. She hurried over to Crane, searching his face. He was sleeping. "Oh, my love," she murmured to him. "How will I ever have a life without you?" She kissed him softly on his forehead. Crane did not stir.

Brain turned to me suddenly, as if she was surprised that I was still there.

"He's asked me to come again tomorrow," I told her.

Brain nodded slowly. "All right. If he wants you to come. It will give me a chance to do errands out of the house. But I don't like the curtains open. Close them before you go." She did not say that she welcomed my visit.

On the walk home, I thought about Crane. I thought about how kind, how touching, his letter to Mrs. Dixon had been. I refused to allow myself to dwell on Brain's rebuff. I thought instead about the privilege I

Revelations

was to have to record Crane's letters. I was excited to discover what his letters would reveal about Crane himself.

I went to Brain and Crane's house every day for the month. Brain would leave the house shortly after I arrived. She said little to me.

Crane's letters revealed his enormous capacity for love and compassion. Letters to friends, acquaintances, and people he had only read about showed that he formed fierce attachments to those whose qualities he admired. He wrote to a poet he had never met, saying his poetry had inspired Crane to become a poet himself. That's how I discovered that Crane had written several poems. "They're not good enough to be published," he said. "But I enjoyed writing them. There are things you can say in poetry that lose their magic when you write them in prose."

Crane's dictated letters contained no recriminations or admonitions. They were full of gratitude and affirmation. A letter to his sister spoke of forgiveness and understanding for their father who had been sullen and aloof, empathy for their mother who had been depressed for most of their childhood, and deep thankfulness for an aunt who had introduced him to philosophy.

Crane dictated letters to Thelma, Andy, and GG, expressing his gratitude for their love and support. He wrote to Thelma, "Your ability to forgive the unforgiveable, your compassion for the frailties of others and the healing powers of your hugs have been inspirational to me. You have made me a better person by your example." To GG, he wrote, "You wonderful happy man, it has been such a pleasure to watch your delight in the smallest of things. You are not distracted by a desire for material goods or ambitions for power. You simply delight in people and nature. You ask for little and you give so much. Thank you for showing me over and over again what's really important in life." He told Andy, "You have been much harder on yourself than you deserve. You fail to acknowledge your tremendous courage in the face of challenges that would have had most of us cowering in the corner. You are an amazingly strong woman who shows all of us how we can overcome the hard things we face. Your example has been such an encouragement to me as I face my death." He asked each of them to care for Brain when he was gone.

By the end of the month of dictation, I had stored 43 letters in my secret box at home.

Malignant Memory

Some days, Crane was too weak to dictate more than a few sentences. Other days, he seemed reinvigorated. He was energetic, passionate, and eager in his dictation. He often laughed at the memories his letters evoked. Many times, he was pensive after the letter was complete, as if the memories had provoked a renewed sense of what he would lose when he died.

After each dictation, Crane and I would talk for a few moments about what he had written. "I never knew you played hockey," I told him after he finished dictating a letter to his former hockey coach. "Yup, but I wasn't that good at it. I was a great skater, but I didn't understand competition. The coach was always yelling at me that my job was not to help the other side." Crane laughed, remembering how angry his coach had been.

Sometimes Crane and I would talk about his dying. He spoke openly about the indignities of dying. "Is there anyone left in Kingsford that doesn't know I am dying? They see me as a dying person, now. Not just Crane, the man." He told me about the things and the people he would miss. My eyes filled with tears as he said, "I will miss you Ba. I will miss seeing where you go in this life. I know there is something special destined for you."

"Ask me anything you like," he said. "When else will you get the chance to ask someone about the experience of dying?" I asked Crane if he was afraid of dying. "Not the death part," he answered, "When you are dead, I don't think you feel things. But I am afraid that as things get harder, I will lose my self-control. I may cry a lot. I may feel sorry for myself. I may drool. I hope I die with some dignity." He was quiet for several minutes. He closed his eyes. I thought he was asleep.

"I think my biggest fear is that Brain won't be able to manage all this. She is shutting out everyone else in our lives because she is desperate to hold onto the lives we once had. I can't do anything to stop the demolition that's happening to my body, our lives. It is a runaway train, spiralling toward obliteration. Neither Brain nor I can stop it. I know that. She is still hoping that she can alter the inevitable outcome."

I asked Crane what he thought would happen when he died. He was silent for a long time. Then he answered. "I no longer believe in an after-life as I was taught as a child. I can't see that there's a heaven—a heaven with streets paved with gold and angels strumming harps.

Revelations

Most people would not like the idea that there isn't a heaven. A heaven that makes all the pain they experienced on earth worth it. And who knows? Maybe I am wrong? Maybe there's a heaven after all. It really doesn't matter. I will find out for myself when I die. In the meantime, I will comfort myself with the idea that I have loved many people. I think I helped create good memories for most of them. I think that I will live on in the memories of the people I have loved. That I will continue to exist because people remember."

Gradually over time, Brain became less guarded, less terse, with me. She waited at the door as I was about to leave, making conversation. It was not the quality of dialogue we used to have when Brain's world was more secure, but I was grateful for any communication between my friend and myself.

Brain confided in me about changes in Crane that she had observed. She asked for my assessment. "He is less pale now, don't you think?" "Do you think he's doing better with his pain? I think so but I just wanted to know what you think." She was visibly relieved whenever I confirmed that I thought Crane was doing better.

Brain never asked about me. She did not inquire about Andy, GG, or Thelma. Crane and I had many conversations about my plans for university. Brain seemed to have forgotten that I was going away to university in the fall. She never spoke of it.

Once Brain said to me, "You and me. We're a team. We know Crane can live, even though the others think he will die." The intensity of her words caused me to take a step backward. It was clear that Brain viewed us as a fortress to forestall Crane's death.

I saw Crane failing in front of us. I knew that we were not sufficient to do what she wished.

CHAPTER FOURTEEN

GRIEF

As the August heat settled in Kingsford, Crane's deteriorating physical state could not be denied, even by Brain. His breath was shallow and smelled of stale cheese. He rarely ate. He drank only when Brain pestered him that he needed fluids and then he took only a few sips. His eyes were glazed. He seemed detached, as if he was no longer really with us.

Crane asked us to call him by his birth name, William. "I used to be called Crane because I was strong. That seems ridiculous now. I can't even feed myself. Call me by the name I was given. Call me William please."

Crane called Brain Margaret. He told me, "These nicknames that we give each other—they put people in boxes. We begin to see ourselves within those boxes. They limit us. Margaret is brilliant and I was strong. We were Brain and Crane. But she has strength that even she is not aware of. She is compassionate, generous, kind, and courageous. She is so much more than a brain. She is strong. I need her to know that now more than ever. I will leave her soon. She needs to know she can survive my leaving."

Crane started calling me Elizabeth. "It's a beautiful name," he told me. He did not explain why he no longer called me Ba.

One afternoon, I was surprised to see Crane sitting upright in bed, waiting for me when I entered the house. Brain had already left. "I have an important letter for you to write today, Elizabeth. I didn't take any of my pain medicine so I could be alert today," Crane announced.

I was pleased to hear the power in his voice. He seemed like the old Crane again. Crane had lived much longer than what the doctor had predicted. Could he be making a recovery?

The letter was addressed to Brain. Crane dictated it slowly, sadly. He watched my response as he spoke.

"My Darling Margaret,

"You will not allow me to talk to you about what has transpired between us. Every time I approach the subject, you leave the room or shut me up. I know it causes you great pain to talk about it, but we need to address what has happened.

"You, my sweetness, need to know that I understand. I forgive you.

"I do not blame you for the events of the past months. I know that because of my illness you were stretched past what any human being should have to endure. I know that you love me mightily. I know that under any other circumstance, you would not have hurt me as you have done."

I stopped writing. I looked at him sharply. What was this about? Brain hurting him? That could not be true. She loved him.

Crane reached out to touch my hand. "This is going to be a very hard letter for you to hear," he said. "I will try to help you understand. You must promise to never, never mention this to anyone."

I nodded, speechless.

"Promise?" he asked.

And again, "Promise?"

I nodded vigorously.

Crane told me to move him on his side. Even though I tried to be gentle, his face contorted with pain as I moved his frail body. "Pull up my pajama top," Crane said. "Look at my back."

I did as he told me. What I saw when I lifted his top caused me to gasp out loud.

There were teeth marks covering the entirety of his back from the neck to the tailbone. The punctures were small, the size of Brain's bite. Some marks were obviously old. The bruising around them was pale yellow and gold. Some were surrounded by black, purple, and blue splotches. Others were red, bloody; they had just recently broken the skin.

I stared at the teeth marks. Comprehension came slowly, reluctantly. Brain, my Brain, was doing this terrible thing to the man she loved. How was that possible? I thought, bizarrely, as I looked upon

Grief

the panorama of bruising and teeth marks, "It's like she's painting a picture of her pain with her teeth."

I could not form words for several minutes. My brain was too crowded with questions, reactions. Why would she do such a thing to the man she loved so dearly? Didn't Crane tell her to stop? Were the bites causing him pain? How could Brain cause him pain? He is so vulnerable, so frail. How could she take advantage of him this way?

Over and over again I said to myself, I hate her. I hate Brain for doing this. Then I said it out loud.

Crane spoke softly. "She doesn't want to hurt me. It's like Thelma and Andy's furies. The anger about what is happening to me and to us, the grief about what has happened and what will happen—it overwhelms her. She lashes out. She lashes out at the one person who she loves best. She knows somewhere deep inside that I will love her no matter what. That I will understand."

He waited for me to respond. I continued to stare at his back.

"Try to understand what it's like for her. We have had a wonderful life together. We love each other deeply. We learn from one another, we encourage one another. We can read each other, understand the meanings of things in each other, we see things that others would not see in each other.

"We know we are exceptionally fortunate to have experienced the kind of love we have known. Margaret will lose that when I die. She will have the memory of our love, but it won't be enough to sustain her when times are bad.

"There's another thing—Margaret has spent her whole life fighting. She fought hard to make a contribution to the world. She has had to fight just for the ability to go to school and to have a job, things you and I take for granted. I have helped her because I can carry her upstairs. I can take her to places that would be inaccessible otherwise. When I am gone, she will have to depend on other people to do those things. She will not be able to stay in the house anymore. She will need to go somewhere, maybe with her father, just to survive. Margaret sees my death as her death, the death of everything she has cared about and valued. She has lost our pets, her job, her privacy, her independence. Soon she will lose me.

"I am disappearing in front of her. I am consumed with my pain.

I am too tired to talk. I don't touch her much anymore. Biting me makes me real again. It's a real connection.

"I know that's hard to understand, but I am asking you to try. You have loved Margaret. She has loved you. She is going to need you when I die. I need to know you will forgive her for this. I need to know that you will continue to love her."

I finally spoke. "Brain taught me to yell at Andy when she has the furies. To make her stop. Do you yell at Brain to stop?"

Crane did not answer my question. "Can you help me get back onto my back?" he asked.

I repositioned Crane on his back. He let out a sharp piercing scream as I moved him. He refused the pain medication I offered him. "I need to be alert right now."

He was quiet for a long time after he took his pills.

Crane continued to dictate the letter. It was a letter of benevolence and love. It ended with, "I understand why you bit me. It was an act of desperation, not of aggression.

"Please my darling, please forgive yourself. Otherwise, the self-loathing will overcome you. It will cause you to withdraw from others. It will make you be less than the amazing woman you are. I would be devastated if that were to happen. Please do not let my legacy be your destruction. Find the incredible strength you have shown so many times in your life and fight against the fear that overtakes you. Tell yourself that my death is the beginning of a renewed you, someone who is even stronger and more resilient than before. Know that you have given me a great gift, the greatest gift of all, by loving me. Know too that I have loved you deeply and completely."

I folded the letter and placed it in an envelope for safe-keeping. Crane asked if I would keep my promise to keep his secret. I nodded, afraid that if I spoke I might unleash the anger and confusion I was experiencing.

Brain arrived home. She wanted to chat about our day. "Did he eat anything when you were here? How was his pain?"

I rushed past Brain at the front door. "I have to help Andy," I said, my head down.

Later, in my bedroom at home, I tried to make sense of what I had discovered that day. I cried to think of Crane being Brain's victim. I

Grief

shook with fury that Brain had done what she did to him. I hated her. I couldn't imagine ever liking her again.

GG came into my bedroom at midnight. He sat at the edge of my bed, holding my hand and looking at me quizzingly, tilting his head as if to ask me, "What's wrong?"

"I can't tell you," I told him. "It's a secret."

GG engulfed me into his puny arms. He held me for a long time while I sobbed. Then he patted the pillow, motioned for me to lie down, and stroked my cheek until I fell asleep. When I woke in the morning, GG was asleep, lying beside Aphrodite curled at the end of my bed. I saw immediately how frail GG had become in the past weeks. I knew that sometime in the future I was going to lose him as well as Crane. I was filled with an inconsolable sadness.

CHAPTER FIFTEEN

LOSS

Crane died in the first week of September. His last week was difficult, unbearable to watch. His pain was unrelenting. His feet and hands became increasingly cold. They were purplish in hue, almost black at the tips.

Crane was stoic whenever he was awake. When he slept under the influence of narcotics, he whimpered and cried. Brain and I wept to hear him suffer as he did. We cried because we were powerless to help him. We cried because of the loss his death would be to our lives.

Brain and I sat with Crane's disappearing self on the night he died. I had not said more than a few words to her since Crane's revelation of the bites. I was deliberately avoiding her. Brain told me that Crane had requested that I stay with her during the deathbed vigil. I agreed to stay for him.

When I came to sit with Brain at the deathbed, Crane had lost consciousness. He barely resembled the hale and hearty man he had once been. He was emaciated, deathly pale. His breathing was laboured. Occasionally, he stopped breathing altogether. Brain and I would watch him closely whenever he did this, willing him to take another breath. We sighed with relief when he made a loud gasp and resumed breathing.

I felt incredibly honoured to be with Crane as he was dying. I willed my strength into him so that he could face whatever lay before him. I prayed for his courage and peace as he exited this world.

I forced myself not to think about the bite marks, Brain's abuse. Brain began to talk to me after we had sat together for a few hours.

Malignant Memory

She told me stories of their life together. She prattled about silly, touching, and perplexing moments in their history together. I did not comment. She did not seem to notice.

At one point, the telephone rang. We did not answer it. I thought, "How can people use the telephone when Crane is dying?" It seemed bizarre that the rest of the world was preoccupied with the ordinariness of life when my beloved Crane was on his deathbed.

Shortly before midnight, Crane died. Brain and I sat silently beside his body for several seconds, unable to acknowledge it was the end. Brain stood up. She fell over Crane's chest, sobbing, begging him to be alive. After some time, Brain told me to telephone Crane's friend, Jim. She told me to go home when Jim arrived. "He's an undertaker. He'll help me. I don't need you here," she said sharply.

I walked home, stumbling down the sidewalk until I reached Andy's house. I opened the door. Andy was in the kitchen. She rushed to hug me, to sit me down and bring me tea. I felt numb, as if I'd never feel again.

The funeral was held three days later. The funeral parlour was packed with mourners. The closed casket was mahogany. I thought it strange that such a beautiful vessel should contain the ugly reminders of the ravages of the disease that had robbed Crane of his vitality. Daisies, Crane's favourite flower, adorned the casket. A white ribbon extended from the bouquet down the side of the casket. It read in red, "Beloved husband, beloved friend."

Andy and Thelma motioned to GG and me that we should go up to the front of the room to give our condolences to Brain. Brain sat in her wheelchair at the corner of the front row. She stared ahead at the casket. She barely acknowledged the well-wishers who came before the funeral service to tell her how sorry they were that Crane had died. Her father, a thin stern-looking elderly man, sat beside her.

Brain sat stiffly as Thelma and Andy hugged her. GG patted her hand. I looked at Brain directly into her eyes, speaking silent thoughts. "I know what you did." Brain averted her glance.

The funeral service contained many tributes to Crane. People of all ages spoke of his integrity, his kindness, and his selflessness. Crane's friend Jim talked about how Crane loved to assist others to make goals when they played hockey together. "He wasn't interested in being the

Loss

one who made the goals," Jim told the audience. "He wanted to be the one that helped others to succeed."

I knew that as the undertaker, Jim would have seen the bruises and marks on Crane's back. I wondered what he thought about them. I wondered if there was an undertaker's code that prevented Jim from telling anyone about the marks. Perhaps Crane had made Jim promise to keep the bites secret.

All the tributes to Crane mentioned how much he had loved Brain. They spoke of Crane as being fulfilled by his love and support of Brain. They told of how Crane knew he was exceptionally lucky to love and be loved by Brain. Crane's sister said, "He always said that he didn't know what he did to deserve Brain. He felt incredibly blessed to have her in his life."

After the funeral, Jim asked me to come to a back room. "Brain wants to see you," he said. "I don't want to see her," I replied angrily.

"Come on," Jim coaxed. "It will only be a minute. Crane would want you to be kind to Brain."

Brain was in the corner of a dimly lit room. Jim led me to a bench in front of Brain. He left us, saying, "You two be alone for a while."

"I am going to live with my father. In Arizona," Brain announced suddenly. She held out an envelope for me. "Crane dictated this letter for you. I told him I would give it to you before I went away. He also gave me a package for you."

Brain's eyes filled with tears. She held the envelope and the package toward me.

I looked at Brain then, noticing for the first time how old she seemed. She was thin, almost wasted. Her eyes were dull. I started to feel sorry for her, for what she had gone through, for what she was facing.

No, I said to myself. She hurt Crane. I willed myself to be angry at her.

"I know what you did to him," I told her with vehemence. "I know what you did. I hate you for what you did. I will never forgive you. Never."

Brain bent her head over her lap. She spoke so softly that I could barely make out what she was saying.

Malignant Memory

"I don't blame you. I hate me too. I will never forgive myself for what I did."

We sat without speaking. Brain's tears splashed on her lap.

Jim came to retrieve Brain. Mourners had gathered at the cemetery for the interment. He told Brain she needed to be there.

I told Andy and Thelma I was not going to the cemetery. GG and I walked home. He held my hand all the way.

I went to my bedroom when I arrived home. I closed the door. GG seemed to understand my need to be alone. He left me alone without protest.

I sat on the edge of my bed and read the letter from Crane.
"Dear one, you are young yet. You have lessons to learn in life. They will be painful lessons at times, but they will be necessary to your growth as a human being.

There is a caution I would like to leave you with. You have a tendency to make heroes out of people you admire, Elizabeth. Hero worship ultimately leads to profound disappointment. The higher you have placed people on a pedestal, the greater the grief you will experience when they inevitably fail to live up to your expectations of them.

There are no perfect people. We are all people, trying our best to cope with what this life brings us. We are not singular in our dimensions. We may be heroic, but we are also flawed and imperfect. It is this confusing paradox that makes us ordinary folk the subject of great literature. It makes us interesting. It also makes us accessible to other people who struggle to be the best they can be while acknowledging that they do not always act in admirable ways.

I hope that you are able to see and appreciate the good in those you admire, despite the ugliness and frailty that will exist in juxtaposition with those worthy qualities. Because, my sweet girl, the same kind of contradictions exist in you as it does in all of us.

I have watched you, dearest Elizabeth, when people have hurt you by their humanness. You put on an armour of steel in defence of the hurt. You have nothing more to do with the person. You are cold and austere when you encounter them.

I would like to tell you in my final words with you that if you don't find a way of forgiving people for their limitations and their offences, your unforgiveness will breed discontent. It will tyrannize your life.

Loss

Please be kind to yourself and learn to let go of the hurts others have caused you by being less than who they should be. Take the sorrow you experience when people disappoint you and learn from it, don't nurture it. For there will come a day when you too will ask for someone's forgiveness.

I thank you for coming into our life. I have loved you deeply.
William"

I sat on the edge on my bed, reading and re-reading his letter. At first, I was angry, defensive. Why should I forgive people who had done despicable things? People should not be forgiven for cruelty and unfairness. Brain certainly should not be forgiven. She had made a dying man suffer because of her abuse.

Then I was engulfed in grief. I had lost a dear friend, an exceptional person who had influenced my life in so many profound ways.

There was a knock on the door. I pretended not to be at home, hoping the person would go away. But GG went to the door and opened it.

It was Hannah, a softer, gentler Hannah, but my Hannah all the same. Hannah sat with me, holding my hand, for a long time. She said little. "I know how much he meant to you," was all she said.

After several minutes, Hannah announced that she had to go home. "We live here now, my daughter and I. Down the street from you and Andy. I will call you tomorrow and we will catch up." She paused at the front door. "I should never have cut you out of my life. It was stupid of me. I hope we can be friends again?"

I nodded, suddenly exhausted from the day's happenings. I lay down on my bed to sleep. GG lay beside me, stroking my hair. Aphrodite curled up in a ball at the foot of the bed.

When sleep came, many hours later, I dreamed of a bear howling at the end of my bed, Thelma's bear.

I woke up, drenched in sweat, my cheeks wet with tears.

I opened the package from Crane the morning after the funeral. It contained a letter and a diary. The letter said,

"Dear Elizabeth,

Many years ago your grandfather befriended a young man who was struggling with his purpose in life. That man was me. Your grandfather taught me much. He provided me with a father figure who, unlike my biological father, was loving and supportive. Shortly before

Malignant Memory

he died, your grandfather gave me his diary. He said it contains some information that might be helpful to members of his family one day. He asked me to keep it in safekeeping. He said I would know if the contents of the diary ever needed to be shared with anyone.

I am entrusting you with his diary now. You can decide if you should share it with anyone else.

Please know that I find in you many of the wonderful attributes that your grandfather possessed. I trust that you will use them to do good in this world.

Love always, your friend, William."

I read the diary, all 306 pages, in one sitting. Grandfather's writing was funny, compelling, insightful, and thoughtful. It often brought me to tears. I found myself wishing once again that I had known him in person.

I laughed when I read of Mrs. Willoughby, a woman who had come to the appliance store where Grandfather worked. Mrs. Willoughby had tried to convince my grandfather that she should get a cut in the cost of a wringer washer. She told him she got her arm caught in a washer. She had purchased the washer from another store the previous year. She thought that her accident justified a reduction in the cost of a new washer from Grandfather's store.

I said out loud, "Yes, that's so true" when Grandfather expressed his concerns about his son George at age 12. "He has received too much attention, too much adoration, from his mother and his teachers. He has never known failure, only success. He succeeds in everything he does and without much effort. He now believes that any goal is possible if he just wants it enough. I worry that sooner or later he will come face to face with the brutal reality that desire and ability are not enough in this world. I lay awake nights thinking about how he has few skills or even the motivation to face the hard times that will inevitably come to him."

I cried when Grandfather shared his suspicions that he had tuberculosis. "My cough is ever-present. It is especially horrific at night. Henrietta complains that it keeps her up at night. Even George commented this morning that he heard me coughing all night. I have been coughing up blood lately. I spit it into my handkerchief so that Henrietta and George do not see. I don't want my dear ones to worry." Later that same day, he wrote, "It turns out that I have TB. I will have to go into the sanatorium. The doctor wouldn't say for how long, but he made a long, grim face when I asked if I would be home by Christmas. I have to break this news to Henrietta and I am dreading it. I know she is vulnerable to the furies when she is frightened. Our neighbour, Bill, died last week of TB. Henrietta will be remembering Bill and all the others we have known with TB when I tell her the news. She fears abandonment more than anything. It hurts me to know how much pain this will cause her."

I gasped in shock and disbelief when I read the final entry in the diary. It read, "Henrietta's brother has been located by the detective I hired to find him. I was going to surprise Henrietta. I imagined how elated she would be to find her brother. She has often told me that she dearly loved her baby brother and would do anything to reconnect with him. Now I know that she must never know what became of him. He is dead. She would be devastated if she knew that he had died shortly after he was taken from the family home. She might think of her father more kindly after she learns the details of what happened, but there is a possibility that she might also be angrier at him for the decisions he made.

I have decided not to tell her. It would be cruel, I think, to share this information with her. It is kinder to leave her with the hope that she may one day see him again. I will keep this to myself."

The entry was dated a week before my grandfather entered the TB sanatorium.

An envelope was pasted to the back cover of the diary. Inside, I found a letter typed on official stationery with the letterhead of a detective agency. The letter was folded around a small black and white photograph.

"Dear Mr. Anderson,

I have conducted the search for Master Edmund Christopher Birch as you requested. I have been able to determine that the subject of interest died on June 13, 1914 at the Home for Imbeciles and the Feebleminded in Albany, New York. Contrary to what your wife, Mrs. Anderson, has told you, Edmund was not an infant when he left the family home. He was diagnosed in infancy as an imbecile with limited intelligence. He was seven years of age when he left his family home.

The superintendent of the Home, Mr. William Gibson, provided access to Master Birch's file (Number 1031). It appears from

Malignant Memory

the correspondence in the files that Master Edmund Birch was brought to the Home ten months prior to his death by his father, George Birch. The father had attempted to find care for his son at several institutions prior to bringing Edmund to the Home.

There was a letter in the file written by a friend of Mr. Birch, Mrs. Ruby Stiller, to the Superintendent. Mrs. Stiller wrote that Mr. Birch had dictated a letter to her because he could not read or write. The letter asked that the Home admit Edmund. It said that Mr. Birch and his wife could no longer provide the care Edmund required. It stated, "The little boy is dearly loved by his parents and his sisters. But we can no longer give him the attention he needs. My wife is dying. She can no longer tolerate the strain of lifting him or caring for him. She cannot bear to make the decision to send him away. I know I must do it for her. I also know that this will mean that she will never forgive me. It breaks my heart to give Edmund to you, but I think this is the best."

There were many letters between the Superintendent and Mr. Birch in the coming weeks after Edmund was received at the Home. Mr. Birch regularly asked about Edmund's health. He inquired when he could visit. The Superintendent wrote short cursory notes that indicated that Edmund was thriving, gaining weight and happy. He discouraged Mr. Birch from visiting his son, suggesting that Edmund might become homesick and unhappy if Mr. Birch were to visit him.

It seems that Edmund was well cared for at the Home. There are notes from the staff describing him as lovable and sweet. They wrote that he loved to listen to music. There was one photograph in the file (enclosed).

On June 3, a letter from the Superintendent to Mr. Birch suggested that Edmund was ill. In another letter later that same week, the Superintendent wrote, "He is having trouble breathing and his feet are swollen with fluid. The physician does not believe that the situation is critical, merely that it is a sign of the heart trouble that these children often have. I remind you that Edmund is very happy at the Home. I do not advise that you visit him at this time as the upset may exacerbate his heart trouble."

There is a copy of the death certificate in the file. The physician indicated that the cause of death was heart failure. I was unable to determine if it was Edmund or another child, a girl, who was buried in

Loss

plot 1031. The girl had the same number as Edmund. Clerical errors are apparently common in the Home's records.

Mr. Birch dictated a letter to the Superintendent two months after Edmund's death. He thanked the Home for their care of Edmund. He wrote that his wife had forgiven him before she died. She had apparently sent Mr. Birch a letter asking him to return home. She indicated in the letter that she understood that he had made the decision to send Edmund away for her sake. Mr. Birch wrote the Superintendent that his wife had died by the time he received the letter.

As you requested, I also interviewed Mr. Birch's eldest daughter, Mrs. Harvey Simpson; she requested that I refer to her as 'Maude'. Maude emphasized that it was clear shortly after Edmund's birth that he was "not right." She indicated that doctors tried to convince her parents that Edmund should be placed in an institution. They said it was kinder to take him out of the family home to be with people like himself.

Maude reported that her mother felt it would be better for Edmund to be surrounded by the love of a family than to be placed in an institution. She stated her mother was devoted to her son. She did not complain when he took over an hour to sip four ounces of milk. She was exuberant when he rolled over by himself at two years old.

Mr. Birch, Edmund's father, made a crib especially for Edmund. Edmund lay in the crib in the front room of the house, in full view of all who entered the front door. Maude said that her mother often proclaimed, "I won't have him put away in another room just because some people are uncomfortable. He's part of our family and he will be treated that way."

Maude said that Edmund was a "sweet child." She told me, "He was almost never unhappy. He would lie in his crib, smiling peacefully, as if he were an angel come to bless us by his presence. He had this habit of touching my check with his palm and looking right into my eyes. He communicated love even though he didn't say a word."

When Edmund was six years old, Mrs. Birch was diagnosed with a serious heart condition for which there was no cure. The doctor told her husband that her only hope to live more than a few months was to rest and to live a stress-free life. The family was warned by Mrs. Birch's physicians that Edmund's care was too taxing for her heart. At the time, Maude lived in Canada with her husband. Daisy, her sister, was engaged to be married and working in a factory. Helen, her younger sister, was a high school student and was away from the house during the day. Henrietta, the youngest daughter, your wife, was only eight at the time.

Henrietta began to share the care of Edmund with her mother. Maude described how joyfully Henrietta assumed this responsibility. "I think she thought of Edmund as her baby. She loved him with a fierce devotion. My mother saw that and she began to rest more, letting Henrietta do what needed to be done. I still remember coming to the house one day. Henrietta was changing Edmund's diaper and she was singing to him. Edmund giggled happily. It was hard to remember that Henrietta was only a year older than Edmund. She seemed like a little mother."

When Edmund was seven, Mrs. Birch became severely ill. Maude told me that her father knew that Mrs. Birch could no longer care for Edmund. Henrietta was not being given the opportunity to go to school because she was the only one available to care for Edmund. Mrs. Birch made it clear that she would never agree to send Edmund away. Shortly after, Edmund and Mr. Birch disappeared.

Maude indicated that at first they did not know where Edmund or her father was. However, a family friend, Mrs. Stiller, confided to her mother that Edmund was in the Home and that Mr. Birch was working out of state to support the cost of Edmund's care. Mrs. Simpson said that her mother forgave her father before she died. She said that her mother sent Mr. Birch some of her books as an indication of her forgiveness.

I trust that this information is sufficient for your purposes. An invoice for my services is enclosed.
Sincerely,
James Purchase, Detective
First Detective Agency."

I stared at the photograph of Edmund for a long time. He was an attractive little fellow, with dark curls that framed his tiny face. He was sitting in a chair with a wooden tray in front of him, belted in the chair to prevent him from falling. He was smiling at the photographer. He looked much smaller than most seven-year-olds I knew.

I wondered what Edmund had thought when he was ripped from his family to go to an institution where he knew no one. I couldn't help thinking that no paid staff, no matter how caring they were, could replace a family who loved him. I shed a few tears when I thought of the poor little fellow dying alone, away from his family. I cringed when I recalled that he had been called an "imbecile."

I wondered if Andy was aware of the diary, if she had found it in the desk and read the truth about her brother. I pretended to be interested in keeping a diary myself. I told Andy I needed advice about how to begin a diary. "Have you ever kept a diary?" I asked her.

She looked up from her knitting, surprised. "No, never," she answered firmly. "I wouldn't want people finding it and reading my secret thoughts."

"Did Father or Grandfather keep a diary?"

"Oh, no. Your father was too busy for that sort of thing. He was always with his friends or playing sports. Your grandfather hated writing. He even hated writing a note on a birthday card. He would never have kept a diary."

I found myself staring at GG one afternoon. He was playing with the dog. I wished I could ask him to fill in the holes of the story. Why didn't he tell his family where he was taking Edmund? Why did he take so long to return to his family? Why didn't Maude tell Andy what she knew? How could she have let Andy believe that GG was evil all these years?

GG returned my stare with a look of puzzlement. "It's nothing," I told him, "just something I wish we could talk about." GG shrugged his shoulders and returned his attention to Aphrodite.

In the end, I gave GG the diary and told him to find a secret compartment in the roll-top desk to hide it. "Don't show me where you put it," I told him. "I don't want to know."

GG looked puzzled, but he did as I asked. He placed the diary in a secret compartment in the old desk.

The roll-top desk remains in my house to this day. The diary is safely ensconced within its secret caverns. I have never looked for it. I did not tell anyone that it existed. I recognized that my dead grandfather had granted me a secret. I kept his confidence.

CHAPTER SIXTEEN

MY SECRET

Hannah says that life is like a bus ride. We ride a bus with the people in our life until it is time to exit. Some people on the bus disembark at stops along the way. Many who leave the bus we never see again.

Sister Margaret Rose got off my bus. I do not know where she is. I asked at St. Theresa's if I could have her address. They claimed not to know where she went.

I keep hoping that I might see Sister Margaret Rose again some day, that our paths will cross again. I wish I could tell Sister Margaret Rose how much she has influenced me. I wish I could thank her.

Sometimes people who have left the bus get on the bus with us once more. That was the way it was with Hannah. I live with Hannah now. Hannah and I are companions, partners, lovers. We are parents to her daughter, Sage.

Hannah writes children's books about bullying and being different. She is dismissive whenever I compliment her on her writing. She refuses to accept my acclamations, although her books have won many awards and significant critical acclaim. She tells me that some of the greatest tyrants throughout history have been experts about the evils of persecution. "It doesn't mean that they haven't engaged in the same evil they say they despise."

Crane got off the bus permanently when he died. His death was followed in later years by that of Aphrodite, GG, Thelma, and finally, Andy. Their death left a hole in my world that I still fall through.

Aphrodite died at the foot of my bed in her sleep. I have had

Malignant Memory

many dogs since her, dogs of pedigree and beauty—but no dog has ever matched Aphrodite in compassion and loyalty. GG died after Aphrodite. He died sitting in his favourite chair in Andy's living room at the age of 93. Right up to his death, he was still able to put his socks on, standing on one foot with his leg sticking out in a right angle in front of him. GG died with his secret intact. Andy never discovered what happened to her brother and why GG had left his family.

Thelma died shortly after GG. Her diabetes had ravaged her body. She had undergone amputations of both of her legs. She was blind. She never complained. Her sense of humour remained intact. She refused to incorporate the regime of diet and insulin that the physicians prescribed. She loved food and she refused to curtail her appetite for it. She was fond of saying, "If it's my time to go, I will go. I've had a good life." She was gracious and caring to the end.

Thelma was buried beneath the sunflowers in her garden. No plaque or monument marks her grave. But many of us carry her memory with us as a precious gift every day of our lives.

Andy was ill for a long time with heart disease. She lived in our home with Hannah, Sage, and me at the end. She was a wonderful support and comfort to us. Sage remembers Andy as a jokester, a happy person who loved to tell stories about her life. She never witnessed Andy's furies. I miss Andy dearly.

Brain died too, but I didn't know that for a long time. I did not keep in touch with her after Crane's death. I don't know how she died. I didn't care about Brain for a long time. I hated her. I was glad she was off the bus.

I busied myself with my life and my studies after Crane's death. Brain moved to Phoenix a month after Crane's funeral. Their little house was sold to a young couple who did not know the sadness that the house contained. I never spoke to Brain again.

Brain did not call to say good-bye to Andy, Thelma, GG, or me when she left Kingsford. Thelma tried to telephone Brain's father, but the phone had been disconnected. None of us received correspondence from Brain or her father.

Thelma said, "She just wants to disappear. She wants to get as far away from the pain of losing Crane as she can. It won't work, but she doesn't know that yet."

My Secret

Brain had commissioned a famous sculptor to fashion an extraordinary gravestone in honour of Crane after his death. The monument was massive, towering over all the other graves in the Kingsford cemetery. It was marble. Ironically, it took a crane to lift it into place.

The gravestone sculpture was a stunningly beautiful woman, standing 12 feet high. She was dressed in the garb of Ancient Greece. A crown of daisies framed her hair. Her face was tender. There were marble tears on her cheeks. Her head was bowed. She was standing on a thick platform made to resemble an open book. The page on one side of the marble book read:

"Here lies the body of William James Foster,
Beloved champion and friend"

The page on the other side was a quote from Plato:

"No evil can happen to a good man, either in life or after death"

Crane's tombstone is now one of the tourist attractions in Kingsford. The monument has become famous. Visitors marvel at the monument's artistry. They often have their photographs taken in front of the Greek goddess. Some have picnics beside the grave.

The passage of time did nothing to lessen my hatred of Brain. Instead, the anger and loathing grew and fermented inside me. When I returned to Kingsford after university, I made a daily pilgrimage to the cemetery where Crane is buried. I would wait until the tourists had gone home, usually right before the cemetery closed for the night, to visit Crane's grave. I would stare at the quote on the marble page, and I would remember the bite marks. I fumed with disgust.

Some time in the times between waking and dreaming, I let go of the anger I felt toward Brain. I forgave her. It began with me recognizing what Brain had contributed to my growth as a person. Over time, I began to think about what Crane's dying must have been like for Brain. I recognized how inadequate I would be to handle the loss of my own dear Hannah. The forgiveness was cemented when I cared for Andy over the course of several months as she was dying.

Andy developed a disease of her heart in her seventies that caused her heart muscle to be flabby and weak. She was unable to tolerate the simplest of activity. Even talking was too much effort for her struggling heart.

Andy came to live in our home so that we could provide the care and support she needed. I was happy to do so. It was my chance to give back some

Malignant Memory

of what she had gifted me in the years before. I think I believed that if I loved her enough, gave her the care she needed, she would live.

It was hard to believe how far Andy had grown in her ability to love and to trust the love of others in her lifetime. The furies had appeared only a few times in the past years. They were apparitions of the former furies. They were minor episodes, easily controlled by Andy herself before she did damage to others. My going away to university, the death of Aphrodite, GG, and Thelma, and having to leave the house she had lived in for so long were tenuous times for Andy. These were occasions for the furies to make themselves known.

Andy was admitted to the hospital nine times one summer. Her care consumed most of my waking moments. Andy needed oxygen in a tank to survive at home. She was dependent on an increasing number of drugs to get through her day. She could not bathe or dress herself. She often woke me from my bed because she could not breathe. Only I could calm her when she believed she was going to drown in the fluids her lungs produced. I existed on little sleep.

I picked Andy up from the hospital after she was discharged at the end of the summer. She was clutching an oxygen mask to her face. She looked tired but happy. I wheeled her wheelchair to the car. I helped her into the car. Andy looked up at me and smiled. "My dear Elizabeth," she said, "I love you."

Andy seemed to have more energy after her hospital stay. She asked Sage about her life. She offered to cut the vegetables for dinner. She ate almost everything on her plate. She was animated when she told stories of me as a younger person. I was encouraged. Maybe the doctors had finally figured out the right combination of drugs so that the Andy I knew would return to us.

I heard Andy call for me from her bedroom later that night. Her voice was frightened, shrill. I ran into her room. She was sitting at the edge of the bed, hunched over, her lips pursed. Her mouth and hands were blue. She wheezed, "I need to go back to the hospital."

I cannot explain what happened. Maybe it was my fatigue. Maybe it was the realization that she was going to die, no matter what I did to prevent it. Whatever the reason, what came out of my mouth was so horrid, so vile, I can barely repeat it to you. It was as if a beast from the pits of hell had overtaken me.

I screamed at Andy. I yelled that she was a burden, that I couldn't take it anymore, that I couldn't stand her being sick all the time. I accused her of not trying to get well, of enjoying the attention. Andy looked down at the floor.

My Secret

She was quiet.

Finally, Andy looked up at me. She said it softly, quietly.

"Elizabeth. You have the furies."

I was so startled that I stopped my tirade against her in mid-sentence. I immediately begged for her forgiveness. I ran to her side, embracing her in a hug. I told her I loved her. I took her to the hospital.

That experience helped me to appreciate the fine line between care and violence, between goodness and evil. Because of what happened on that fateful night, I knew firsthand that when people are overwhelmed by grief and fear, they can do despicable things to the people they love. It was then that I forgave Brain.

I wrote Brain a long letter to her father's address begging her forgiveness for how sullen and judgmental I had been. My letter was returned unopened. "NOT AT THIS ADDRESS" was written across the envelope.

Shortly after, I was walking through the cemetery. I went to Crane's grave as I always did. There beside his grave was a monument for Brain. She had been buried beside him. The small granite stone had not been there the week before.

The monument read, "Here lies Margaret Foster, wife of William Foster." A line below was engraved in italicized script. It was a quote from the Roman philosopher Seneca. It read, "All cruelty springs from weakness."

I knew immediately that the line on Brain's tombstone was in reference to her biting Crane. The realization that she would hate herself so much that she would define herself this way for others to see forever more filled me with such horror that I sunk to my knees at her grave.

I went to see Jim, Crane's friend, that afternoon. Jim had retired from the funeral home. His son had taken over the business. Jim's son told me that Brain had died three months before. Brain had requested that she be buried beside Crane. She had left instructions about the writing on the monument. Jim's son did not know how Brain died.

I returned to the cemetery to stare at Brain's tombstone. I sat on a bench facing her grave, too sad and too ashamed to go home to Hannah.

The secret that I have never acknowledged to another person before this time is this—I never gave Brain the letter from Crane. Brain died without ever reading it.

Malignant Memory

I had the letter from Crane with me at the funeral. I fully intended to give it to Brain. But I did not.

It was a deliberate decision. I was so angry, so vengeful. When I saw her at the funeral home at Crane's funeral, I wanted her to pay for her sins.

I would like to think that I withheld the letter from Brain because I was young, caught up in my youthful need for vengeance. I wanted Brain to pay for what she had done. I wanted her to suffer because I was angry. But I had many chances to give her the letter before she left Kingsford and even after.

I never gave Brain the letter from Crane.

I could have asked Jim to send Crane's letter to her. I know he corresponded with her for at least a few months after the funeral. He told me once that she had commissioned the statue at Crane's gravesite through a letter to him. I could have put an ad in a Phoenix newspaper asking Brain to contact me. I could have asked the municipality of Kingsford where they were sending Brain's pension cheques. I could have forwarded Crane's letter to that address.

I did none of those things. I did not even enclose the letter from Crane when I wrote to Brain asking for her forgiveness.

The disappointment and anger I directed toward Brain can in part be explained by my age. I was 17 when Crane died. The fallacy of perfect beings is easy to nurture when you are young. As I grew older, I had life experiences that taught me about the imperfections we all have.

It is true that I was horrified that Brain could have hurt her dying husband. But my anger toward Brain was directed more at her desertion of me than it was at my disillusionment of her as Crane's loving wife.

I had come to expect that I was central to Brain's universe. I felt betrayed because she abandoned me during Crane's illness. I was angry that she no longer seemed to care about me or my life. She no longer inquired about my life. She restricted my visits. She seemed not to care about me any longer. We no longer were best friends.

I was glad, even smug, that Crane had chosen me to know about Brain's betrayal. It was a secret between us that Brain did not know. In my adolescent mind, I believed that I had assumed an equal or greater importance to Brain in Crane's life because he shared this secret with me.

My Secret

I was the good one, the one who could be trusted with the secret. She was the evil one, the one who bit him.

If only life was that simple. So black and white.

Youth does not explain why I never gave Brain Crane's letter when I was no longer young and when I had forgiven her for biting Crane. I knew that Brain should have Crane's letter many years before she died, but I was too embarrassed to admit that I had not followed Crane's instructions. He had specifically asked me to give the letter to her after he died. It had been important to him that she receive it. I ignored what he had asked.

I think, too, that after I forgave Brain for biting Crane, I was ashamed of my pettiness, my jealously. I could not figure out how to give Brain the letter without exposing what I had done. I could not face up to my own cruelty, my vengefulness, my frailty.

I rationalized for many years that Brain probably realized Crane forgave her without seeing the letter. He had always loved her so deeply. Surely forgiveness was inherent in such a love. Brain would have realized that he forgave her.

I thought that perhaps Brain had come to the realization herself that what she had done to Crane was an act of despair. It was forgivable because her desperation came from knowing the love of her life would die. It was love, not malice, that caused her to bite him.

I thought she might realize over time that the biting was forgivable because she was overwhelmed by being alone in the experience of watching Crane die. All her life, she had resisted dependency on others because of what it would imply about her limitations. She was ill-equipped, when Crane lay ill, to let others know that she was scared, hurting, and vulnerable. We who loved her could have helped Brain more than we did when Crane was ill. We assumed that she wanted to be independent because she said that is what she wanted.

The words on Brain's simple gravestone confronted me with a painful truth. Brain thought of herself as weak and cruel because she had bit Crane. She thought that the act of biting him on his deathbed was unforgiveable. She had never known that Crane forgave her. And perhaps because she did not experience his forgiveness, she never was able to forgive herself. That beautiful

Malignant Memory

human being who gave so much for others died feeling undeserving of his love.

It is my fault. I chose not to give her Crane's letter.

I have struggled to forgive myself for what I did, for ignoring Crane's request, for failing to share his letter with Brain. The secret has haunted me. I have never been able to tell anyone before this, not even Hannah.

Hannah is fiercely loyal to Brain. She feels that way for many reasons, but particularly because it was Brain who sold one of her mother's paintings, a Tom Thompson painting of autumn leaves, to pay for Hannah and her mother to live in Toronto during Hannah's confinement.

I remember asking Brain where the Thompson painting was. It was her favourite. It had hung in her living room for as long as I could remember. "Sometimes we need a change," was her reply. I stared at the replacement, a mediocre version of the streets of Paris, and wondered how she could have given up the hauntingly beautiful Thompson painting for such a lifeless image.

Hannah believes that Brain was a heroine. I am afraid that if she knew what I had done, if she knew that I had not given Brain the letter that might have provided Brain some relief from her torment, Hannah would not forgive me. I cannot bear the notion that Hannah would be disappointed in me, even ashamed of me. I cannot share my secret with Hannah.

Coming face to face with my own duplicity in sharing my secret with you has been painful and humbling. Crane was right when he said that there would come a day when I needed to be forgiven. I have struggled for a long time with what I did to Brain and Crane. I don't want to forget what I did. I only want to learn from it, to be a better person because of what it taught me.

My hope is that sharing my secret with you will help me to forgive myself.

EPILOGUE

I am a grateful person these days. I am profoundly grateful for the teachers in my life. Their lessons were not always easy, but they have shaped the best parts of who I have become. Their legacy is realized every day in my life.

I am thankful to Sister Margaret Rose. I teach on the reserve by Kingsford now. I teach Cree children. I am a popular teacher but not an easy one. I demand excellence. My appeal to the students I teach is in part the same approaches that Sister Margaret Rose used in her classroom. I am famous for my corny jokes in the classroom. The hair restorer with a permanent wave is one of the children's favourites.

I am grateful for the lessons I learned from Andy, GG, and Aphrodite. They taught me much about perseverance, true beauty, and the endless opportunities we have in life for renewal and forgiveness.

I am reminded every day about Thelma and her friends who shared their stories of residential school with me. I once fancied myself as someone who would write great books about residential schools, books that would reveal the colossal wrongs that were committed in those institutions and by our nation. Thelma and her friends showed me that I can be a sympathetic onlooker, but the story of residential schools and their impact is not mine to tell. Now I help equip the children I teach with the skills they need to make their stories known to the world.

I am grateful for Brain and Crane. When the youngsters I teach ask me how I know so much about books, how I could quote them so easily, I tell them about the freedom I experienced as an alienated child when Brain and Crane taught me that you are never friendless when you are a reader of books.

I learned a great deal about loss and love in my relationship with Brain and Crane. Now I am fiercely committed to providing resources and services not only for people who are dying, but also for their families. I fight to ensure that no family member would be so overwhelmed as they faced their inevitable loss that they resort to abuse of the dying person.

I am indebted to Hannah. Her ability to surpass the tragedy of the rape and the prejudice she faced because of her difference has been an inspiration in my life. I have had a tendency to think that I am the victim when bad things happen to me. Hannah thinks that bad times are an opportunity to gain strength. She says, "Shit happens. You have to learn to wrestle with the shit, to go on despite it, to wipe yourself clean of it; otherwise, you get covered in the stuff. And you begin to think you are the shit others say you are."

I am grateful to you. Sharing my secret with you has been a painful but rewarding experience. It has helped me to become a better guardian of others' secrets, to be a more open and less judgmental secret keeper.

Sharing my secret with you has liberated me from much of the menace that the secret has caused in my life. I am now free of the wariness, the exhausting vigilance, that was necessary in order to keep the secret hidden from others. Giving you my secret to guard has allowed me to go on with my life, to put the secret in its proper place and to move past it. I will always regret that I was not more understanding of Brain's pain. I will always have remorse that I did not do as Crane requested and give Brain his letter. But I see the secret as part of my past. I have learned from it. I will be a better person because of it.

I have thought a great deal lately about Thelma's story about the bear who roared. Over time I became convinced that the bear was a metaphor for a person with a secret. I thought that I, as the guardian of people's secrets, pulled the "thorn," the secret, from their paw. I granted them peace because I relieved them of their secret.

I see now that the bear was me. The thorn represents the judgments that I made of the people who shared their secrets with me.

Epilogue

When I judged, I roared my verdict of the secret teller's confessions.

Secret tellers regularly observe my reactions during their confessions as a litmus test of how horrid or inadequate they are. They scan my face, particularly my eyes, for any sign of repulsion, fear, or condemnation. In the past, they found no such evidence. I had learned to mask my disgust and displeasure. I have always told secret tellers that it is not up to me to judge someone else.

It was not true. I did judge.

The judgment I directed toward secret tellers has caused me great pain over the years. In the past, the firsthand knowledge of people's secrets, the realization of how rarely people are who they say they are—or who they appear to be—made me reluctant to trust. It caused me to be spiteful, unrelenting in my hatred, when I learned that Brain had abused Crane. It caused me to abandon Brain when she needed me most.

Some secret tellers ask if I despise them for what they revealed. Some ask for my forgiveness. Thanks to what I have learned in sharing my secret with you, I now respond that I see the secret tellers and their stories as connected to me, part of me, not separate from me. I recognize myself—my motivations, my fears, my failings, my contradictions, and my limitations—in the secrets of others. I know now that although I may not have done what they confess, I am capable of doing the same things. Judgment is irrelevant in such a context.

I see now that my calling is as the keeper of secrets, not the judge of secret tellers. I no longer bear the thorn of judgment.

I learned this in telling you about my secret. I learned this in forgiving myself.

The bear now rests in peace.

BIOGRAPHY

Barbara Paterson was an adult before she discovered that her dearly beloved grandmother had grown up in an orphanage. This information helped her to make sense of the uncontrollable rages that her grandmother often experienced. Later, in her work as a nurse with residential school survivors and people who experience devastating illnesses, she recognized that the ravages of extreme grief are often revealed in the damage committed to self or others. She has been the recipient of several prestigious awards, such as the 3M Teaching Excellence Award, the Queen Elizabeth Diamond Jubilee Medal and Canada's Most Powerful Women Award, for her work as a university educator and her research on chronic illness. Currently, she is retired. She lives in Steinbach, Manitoba with her husband, George.